The Bog Maiden

David Pilz and George McAdams

The Bog Maiden

by David Pilz and George McAdams

Published by PilzWald
P.O. Box 876
Corvallis, Oregon 97339
www.pilzwald.com

Printed by CreateSpace, An Amazon.com Company

ISBN 13: 978-0-9981137-2-2

"Strange things happen in the bog. There will always be some ambiguity." Lynnerup smiles. "I sort of like the idea that there's just some stuff we'll really never know."

Niels Lynnerup
University of Copenhagen
Quoted in "Tales from the Bog" by Karen E. Lange
National Geographic, September 2007

Contents

Acknowledgements

Many friends and relatives read early drafts of the manuscript and provided helpful comments.

Former copy editor for the Seattle Post-Intelligencer, Ron Post, applied his talents to the novel, improving it greatly.

I extend my gratitude to Paula Fong who created original artwork for use in the novel. Her web site is: http://www.prfong.com

Prologue — Unreachable

ACCURSED HOPE!

How long has my spirit been bound to this stinking bog? Even the grains of sand in the oozing muck would be easier to count than the cycling seasons of my miserable entrapment. Days never move, but drag from moment to dreary moment. The nights are insufferable. My trapped spirit takes on enough form in the droplets of pre-dawn fog that I can physically sense my bleak and tedious surroundings. The putrid scum that clings to my feet and calves. The penetrating chill and ceaseless rain. The vaguely defined bushes, insect-eating plants, and mats of thick moss that line the edges of the bog … all drab-colored even in the brightest moonlight. The twisted trees draped with decaying moss, sickly luminous lichens, and shelf rot-fleshes sprouting from heartwood decay. Most importantly, that unreachable grove of oak trees harboring the jumping ground-fleshes of my unreachable deliverance. Is he still there? I feel his needy spirit each wane-sun and during times of threat, but cannot touch him, cannot not know his mind. Can he sense my torment? Does he share it?

Assuredly, the endless stretches of boredom and

depression have been broken a few times when the bog has invoked my curse and summoned me to fulfill my doom. I have been enjoined to protect this backwater, the sacred grove, and its denizens against all threats; storms, meteors, quaking earth, rising seas, floods, fire and drought. My tribe also continues to live on the nearby dune-lands, on the borders of the sea, and occasionally I will catch glimpses of distant descendants as they pass the edges of this wretched bog. Mostly they avoid these gloomy and ill-fated quagmires. The rituals are lost, the chain of memory broken, the paths faded. Why should they tempt the restless spirits of forgetting when there is nothing for them to gain?

So the bog, the grove, the rot- and ground-fleshes, my spirit, and my spell persist down the long passageway of ages. So too, I pray, does my ancient lover.

Now, this time, it seems different. The new threat is not a force of this world but comes from the twisted minds of strange new men. I feel the bog invoking my curse; calling me once again to its defense. Suddenly a young man, descended from the ancient hill tribes, actually ate the jumping ground-flesh! If only one of the strange ones had not come and chased him off!

Will he try again? Can he learn to follow the ritual paths? Can he discern the methods of our release? Is there another chance for us? Can we possibly be together again? Might I finally be released!?

ARRWWAHH! ACCURSED HOPE!

Chapter 1 — Ole's Date

ugs knew that his old friend and fellow cranberry farmer, Ole Gorseman, would never reveal the details of what happened on the night in question. It didn't matter. The dippy high school girls had seen and talked enough. The story was now common knowledge among the inhabitants of the little town of Danemark on the southern Oregon coast. Maybelle, the town gossip and soon-to-be-crowned Berry Queen, made sure of that. Of course, not everyone, especially Bugsy, credited the embellished tale with veracity, but it was a good listen; and anyway, what else would account for Ole's seeming change of heart?

"Ya know, Ole, they say she traps men vidth her voice, sorta like a deep sexy vhisper in der minds, an' den da dern fools can get schtuck in da bog vhen dey vaddle outa her in a trance."

"Bug off Bugsy! I ain't saying what happened. It's hard enough being a cranberry farmer without spending your nights chasing hippy Indian kids and a gaggle of giggling high school girls out of the wild parts of your farm. What if one of them was to drown on my property? Fine mess, that'd be. And, would you please lay off that lame feigned

Norwegian accent!"

Ignoring Ole's protests, Bugs continued, "Jah, vell, ya know dey jus' come around because dat particular bog is so derned eerie. Haunted mayhap, even sensuent like in one o' dem sci-fi movies with aliens, an all."

"Crap, Bugsy, I don't care if that bog, or the ghastly old grove next to it, is sentient or what. I don't even care how that, that … what did the girls call it … 'alluring apparition' … I don't even care how her sexy voice controls your mind, I jus…."

"Der! See! Ya admit it! Ya did hear her voice in your head! I knew ya was holdin' back, Ole!"

Ole knew that further conversation with Bugsy on this topic would just leave him open to more truth mining by his old friend and staunch purveyor of spooky yarns. Frankly, he really did not want to talk about what he had experienced that night in the bog. Although Ole usually wouldn't deign to ask the question he had in mind, he felt the subject needed changing.

"So, Bonny thinks I should ask Sally to the festival, eh?"

Bugs and Bonny Sopp had been married as long as anyone could remember. In that regard, Bugs was the antithesis of Ole, but Bugs, on his own, would never rib Ole about his choices. Garrison Keillor was right. Some men were born to be Norwegian bachelor farmers. Bonny, on the other hand, was not content to let other people decide their own fates and saw it as her mission in life to ensure that every deserving eligible bachelor friend of theirs had abundant opportunities to discover the fulfillments of marital bliss that she and Bugs enjoyed. Ole was one of her

few remaining challenges and certainly the most stubborn.
Still, Bonny did not feel comfortable pestering Ole directly
about dating either. That duty fell to Bugs, with Bonny's
persistent prompting. So when Ole asked about Sally, Bugs
jumped right in, knowing Ole had eased his way and Bonny
would be pleased about their conversation.

"Ja, schure, vhy not? Jeez, Ole, Sally is vun fine and
vivacious lass. Ya know dat. An hey, ya ain't no spring
chicken no more neither, eh?"

"Yeah, but you know what they say about divorced
gals, Bugs: damaged goods, too much baggage."

"Kripes Ole, an ya ain't got no baggage? Heck-n'-den-
some, dat dastardly fog bog is a milestone around yer whole
dern life! An' it seems ta have a feminal incantation no less!
An' sultry ta boot!"

"Chuck you, Bugsy! You know what I mean. The way I
heard it, Sally was dumped by her hubby because she wasn't
outgoing enough for him. Insufficiently adventurous! How
is that supposed to make one feel? What a jerk."

"Ja, ya heard right, but she knew she vus jus' a country
gal. It vus her bum boo-boo dat she up and married some
fancy tree scientist dude outa Oly. All she ever vanted ta do
vus ta tend her garden and cook scrumpdillyicious meals.
Dat jerk vus traipsing off ta da mountains with his uppity
wino friends every chance he got. Vhen Sally stayed home,
da scene vus jus ripe for marital infantdelities on his part.
At least his arseholiness fessed up and called it quits afore
Sally got trompled by a hole herd o' lies, or vurs yet, dey
had kids dat vould complicate de divorce. So … mayhaps
Sally ain't ta keen on men right now, but Bonny says she's a
mite lonely nonedaless. Bonny vould know, ya know—she

n' Holly chat a mite bit."

"OK, OK, Bugs. I'll get in touch with her. She might even be able to fend off some of the inquisitory rumormongers I'm likely to run into at the festival this year."

"Vell, I don' know about dat. Seems da buzz is flyin' dick as a ocean fog in summer right now, and not just about dat bog maiden neither, but get dat new-fangled ear-crab outa yer pocket and give her a jingle right now!"

"OK, Bugs, OK!"

Ole didn't much care for the notion of being continuously in touch with potential customers via a smart phone. Heck, until recently, there wasn't even sufficient microwave tower coverage on this part of the Oregon coast to bother with a simple cell phone. His business relied on keeping far-flung customers happy, however, and they seemed, more and more, to demand anytime access to his private life. Whatever happened to business hours? Oh well, he got out his ear-crab and searched for the number Bonny had texted him earlier in the day. Of course, Bonny was quite up-to-date with any technology or communication method that facilitated matchmaking. She had included a nice picture of Sally.

It was around dusk on a cool, late-August evening. Ole and Bugsy were strolling along a berm separating two soon-to-be-swamped bogs that were blushing a cherry red hue with almost-ripe crops of *Vaccinium macrocarpon*, the North American cranberry. Of Ole's 400 acres of cranberry fields, this was his favorite berm stroll. The linear mound bisected two of the oldest bogs on his property, both still producing from his granddad's first plantings of the locally-bred

Stankavich variety back in 1916. Tradition had it that Stankevich (spelled variously) crossed the eastern cranberry of commerce with a local bog berry species to develop the variety, but plant breeders and geneticists with whom Ole had conferred felt a cross with native *Vaccinium* species was unlikely. McFarlin, the crotchety, hardened, cranberry breeder from back East, might have planted cranberries locally as early as the 1890s. Then along comes unsuspecting Stankiewicz who makes his cross with some plants that McFarlin points out growing "wild." All the while, McFarlin is snickering about his prank. Ole's dad, Bert, had never paid much mind to granddad's tall tales, so the story got a little murky by the time Ole inherited it. Whatever. The old family bogs and the Stankavich variety still produced early and well each season. Prank or no, it was a productive, tasty and profitable variety.

As they walked westward toward the Pacific, the sun has already hazed out into the low western Pacific fog banks of summer. He found it hard to concentrate on finding Sally's number in the ear crab's menu, what with his rambling thoughts of the old "stanky" bogs, a frenzied flock of geese honking their pre-autumnal raucousness overhead, and other seasonal changes nibbling at the edges of his senses. But find and punch it he did. Ole was nothing, if not competent. He was, therefore, one of the most successful and prosperous cranberry farmers on the west coast.

As Sally's number rang, their stroll brought them into view of the wild bogs beyond, and suddenly Bugs crouched to the ground to inspect tracks. Distracted, Ole just barely heard Sally pick up.

"Oh, ah…Hi! This is ah… Ole Gorseman…" What the heck was Bugsy inspecting so gull derned carefully?

"Hi Ole. I know yer voice. Long time no hear, though. Nice of ya to call."

Sally's voice was melodious, smooth, and downright, well… down-home. Ole was now doubly distracted by Bugsy's growing snoop-enthusiasm and Sally's intent attention to why Ole might be calling. He didn't even think of lead-in small talk.

"Ahh, yeah. So, ah, I was wonderin', Sally. Would ya maybe like to go to the festival with me this year? I mean, I don't mean to be pushin' you or nothin', but well, Bonny said…"

If good-natured giggling could be an ear-crab ring-tone, Ole was sure he heard it in the tone of Sally's reply, but it wasn't mocking. She just sounded pleasantly amused. Bugsy sounded exactly the opposite as he scrambled along the ground, probing, grunting, and mumbling ersatz Nordish ümlauts.

"Sure Ole, I would be delighted to accompany you to the grand fest this year. Why for berry's sake not?"

Such a question invited an immediate affirmative answer, but wouldn't you know, that is when the perturbed nutria decided Bugsy's schnozz was sniffing too close. The resulting confrontation left Bugsy with a bleeding bitten nose, way wide eyes, and a very muddy butt. Ole stumbled over the sparring berm critters, rolled on the berm path, jumped upright, caught the flying ear-crab in mid-air, and burst out laughing before he realized Sally might be a bit confused by the interruption. Sally, for her part, just shook her head and tried to interpret the aural mayhem on the other end of the line. Fortunately, being a country gal, she was patient.

Finally Ole caught his breath, suppressed his mirth, and panted back on the line. "I am so sorry, Sally. I'm walking along with Bugsy here, and all the sudden he's snooping along the ground like a trail hound. Then this…"

"Don't!" Sally said. "Tell me in person. I want to see you describe it with your hands too. So now I guess we simply must to go to the festival together."

Ole smiled real big inwards. Maybe hobnobbing with Sally might be kinda fun after all. He had known her since childhood but had not seen her for years. She seemed real comfy right now.

"Great! Pick ya up at 6 two Fridays from now, OK? Yer staying at yer mom's place, right?"

"Perfect, Ole. Thanks so much for callin'. Oh, and tell Bugsy that snoopers can get nipped. See ya."

Ole's grin broadened as he offered his dejected friend a hand up.

"So what were you so earnestly scouting out there on the berm you cub?" Ole poked Bugs.

"Don' give me dat crapola, Ole. Dis here is a veritable highway of high school girl tracks, along vid da prints of two hefty guys trampled undaneath. One sure as shucks looks like yer bootprints, dude."

Ignoring his friend's deteriorating accent, he replied, "Bugs, I live here. I work here. I walk all over the place here. You think I can keep all the trespassers out? Get a life. Bug Off," he said for the umpteenth millionth time. They headed back in silence through the deepening dusk to the medicine cabinet to search for anti-nutria-incisor-bacterial cream.

∫

Ole always did like Sally's last name. There it was in bright, light, almost florescent, freshly painted, green letters on her mom's graying and rusted mailbox at the end of the pine-shrouded lane, DARLINGTON. The family had settled here in the early 1870s shortly after the Rogue Indian Wars. Whether or not the family really was distantly related to William Darlington, the Pennsylvania botanist and congressman for whom the signature plant of the coastal dune bogs was named, did not really matter. Darlington was a nice name and the insectivorous pitcher plant, *Darlingtonia californica* was a very cool plant. Sally's eccentric mother, Holly, still grew a few pitcher plants in the artificial swampy pond next to the mailbox.

Ole had actually helped make the pond when he was a teenager looking for odd jobs. After shoveling out a broad bowl of sand near the entrance to their driveway, he had lined the shallow pit with plastic and pinned it down with rocks and sand around the edges. One side was left a little lower so fresh water could be slowly flushed through the pond with a constantly dripping hose that fed into the high end. Then he had covered the bottom with layers of sand, peat moss and gravel. Finally, he, Holly, Sally, and his dad Bert had gone out to collect *Darlingtonia* rhizomes from around the spooky natural bog in the back 40 of his dad's cranberry farm. Holly and Bert had worn hip waders to get out to the pitcher plants on the fringe of the bog. Sally and he had reveled in the goo around the margins, getting soggy and muddy while collecting the rhizomes their parents had tossed to them. In spite of the dazzlingly beautiful spring day, Ole recollected that they had all felt a little weird about what they were doing, almost as if someone were watching. Not so much that they might have defiled a special place; they had only taken a few rhizomes and left a few tracks. More like they wondered what they might be spreading. "Ooga Booga!" the kids teased each other.

Anyway, Ole was pleased to see that Holly had continued to maintain the pitcher plant patch by the mailbox. The only substantial change was the growing collection of glass floats, rusted crab pots, weirdly-shaped driftwood, garden gnomes, exotic rocks, mushroom-themed statuettes, and other eccentric lawn ornaments. Holly's neighbors, it seemed, thought her driveway entrance was an appropriate collection point for such beach detritus and ornamental oddities. Holly did not dissuade them.

Ole did his best to navigate his dark blue 1997 Ford diesel pickup truck down the narrow driveway without leaving ruts in the mossy sand bordering the two gravel tracks, avoidance of which was sort of a neurosis with native Oregonians. He needed a big rig for the farm, but this lane was designed for small cars and it had then been left to narrow over time with encroaching shrubbery on either side.

Oh, well, a few scratches on the sides of his pickup no longer mattered. That is why Ole liked middle-aged vehicles. Still reliable, but not worried about their looks.

All the way over, in fact for several days now, he had been trying hard not to think too much about his upcoming date with Sally. Jeez, when was his last official date? It might actually even have been with Sally, as sorta-friends-like, back in high school. Being not naturally prone to nervousness, Ole nevertheless could swear that there might be butterflies hatching in his guts. That public broadcasting TV special about exotic foods of the world he watched a few nights ago didn't help much.

The Darlington residence was nested deep into a brushy forest of contorted shore pines, down an obscure gravel lane just west of Highway 101 and just north of the small burg of Langlois. No doubt, when the house was built back in the 1930s, the surrounding land was newly cleared sand dunes with just a smattering of small pine saplings and incipient brush-fields. Trees don't get too tall growing in the strong salt winds whipping across these infertile coastal sand dunes, but the forest they formed quickly grew dense and craggy-looking. Holly and Sally's family abode was more of a fancy cottage or beach bungalow than a real house. It had charm in plenty, which partially compensated for certain structural defects that Holly's long-deceased carpenter husband had not anticipated would be so salient in this sodden maritime climate.

Presumably they didn't do a lot of entertaining. Ole barely had room to turn his truck around in the front gravel patch without dinging their cars.

I might be a few minutes early, Ole thought, but I just couldn't drive any slower. Not that Sally would likely mind his slightly premature arrival. He remembered her and her family as punctual, and he guessed (or hoped) she might be a little nervous too.

When Ole stepped down from his truck seat, the family dog started barking; their cat stood up on the porch railing, raised its back hairs in a menacing stretch, and hissed; and a couple of ink-black, ostensibly-perturbed crows lifted off with a duet of obnoxious cawing from a moss patch that served as the lawn. All a might sensitive, he thought.

In an effort to calm his nerves, Ole concentrated on the lovely sea-scent born on the mist floating in through the darkening pines. As he climbed the porch stairs, Holly opened the door and greeted him as if he were a long lost prodigal son by embracing him in a bear hug worthy of a mother grizzly.

"OLE! It is so darn good ta see you again. How long has it been? Jeez-la-wheese, I hear you are one of the most hottin-tottin cranberry farmers around now! Jus' concentratin' on nuttin' but, eh?"

"MOTHER!" Sally rescued Ole with.

"Alright dear. It is just so good to see this fine lad again. It's been sooo long! An' us not getting too many visitors an' all, I just got a little bit carried away is all, right Ole? An' you being so kind as to – "

"Mom!" This time Holly clammed up and just gave Ole another lesser, but warmer hug, and a generous smile.

Ole's concern about what to say when he arrived had quickly dried up (unlike most things on the coast). Although he felt he was still the spotlight of attention, and in particular the focus of Holly's hopes, neither of them in any way really made him feel uncomfortable. The mother-daughter tit-for-tat had all been in good humor, and gee-wiz if Sally didn't look fine! No one had ever accused Sally of lacking style. Her attire was mostly simple and modest, but highlighted with a few apt touches of subtle flair that suggested she fully intended to enjoy herself. Wow. She was decked out sweet for the evening and had a smile stretching from Hawaii to Nebraska.

Of course, Sally and he couldn't proceed to the festival without visiting a while with Holly, but that was part of the reason Ole had shown up early. Folks that know each other adjust their timetables accordingly. Actually, it was very pleasant catching up on events and news with these two lovely women, sitting in a funky kitchen in a dilapidated old cottage on the dunes. Not once did either of them mention the night on the bog. What a relief. He could have stayed all evening. Still, he knew his presence was much anticipated at the festival, as did both of these fine ladies. That, he was not looking forward to, at least not entirely. The festival was always fun, and he didn't get out much, so it was a pleasure to see old friends, but this year he knew he was going to be mercilessly ribbed about the "Incident at the Bog" and about his date, Sally. Oh well ....

As Sally and he left the Darlington cottage, Ole was already sneezing from cat dandruff, the dog was rubbing against his leg with apparent infatuation, and the crows strutted across the hood of his truck, proud of their deposits. Sally, oblivious, just held his arm and swayed as she walked with him to the truck. This is too much, Ole thought. Alas, the evening beckoned. Might as well dive in.

∫

Between his brain and his mouth, the words of Ole's invective got swapped out quickly in deference to Sally sitting next to him in the cab of his pickup.

"Those barnacle-sucking mother pheasant pluckers!" Ole swore instead and then blushed. In his peripheral vision he noted Sally glancing at him, but the corner of her mouth seemed to be curved upward slightly with a hint of amusement.

"Why do small town rumor mills have to be so flabbergasted in-your-face!?" he snarled.

They had just pulled into the parking lot of the decrepit old Woodmen of the World Hall where the Berry Festival opening dinner, coronation, and dance was traditionally held. There above the door, illuminated by upward-pointing, directional lights, was the banner displaying the theme of this year's celebration. In blood red, curlicue, capital letters was the slogan ALLURING MAIDENS OF THE BERRY BOGS. The words overlaid a blown-up Google-Earth view of the area's cranberry (rectangular) and natural (bacteria-shaped) bogs. Over one of the natural bogs, someone had hand-painted a wispy-gray, ghostly-looking, sexy, female apparition rising up from the water, dripping water from strands of clinging moss on both shoulders.

Ole had been amazed at how snuggly Sally had been on the way over. She didn't sit on the far side of the cab seat like a girl on a first date. She slid right over to the middle of the seat, next to Ole, practically inviting him to put his arm around her, which he naturally did. Jeez, just like high school, but relaxed and cozy.

Now, as the bristling Ole used both arms to swing the pickup around in the parking lot, Sally just gave his arm a little jab with her elbow and said, "I think it's kinda cool, and someone obviously put a lot of work into it."

15

In the deepening gloom of dusk, the decaying Woodmen Hall
had a haunted appearance.

"Someone, ja," Ole growled, "and that someone is the gaggle of giggling high school girls led by the supreme rumor monger and soon-to-be Berry Queen, Maybelle Tattleton. I know the Queen-in-Waiting is usually allowed to pick the theme for the festival, but I heard tell that the Berry Theme Committee just handed the whole shebang over to Maybelle and her cohorts this year. Gahds! I wish they had never followed Johnny out to my bogs that night!"

Sally showed her good common sense and empathy for Ole's anxiety by not following up on that comment. Ole appreciated her tact.

In the deepening gloom of dusk, the decaying Woodmen Hall had a haunted appearance. Constructed of readily available but perishable wood, it had seen much better days. Built in the typical rectangular, tall box, flat-roofed, architectural style of the period, it exuded an almost see-if-we-care challenge to a climate characterized by ferocious winter winds and torrential deluges. The building's thick layers of white paint were peeling yet again, to say nothing of the consequences of poor roof drainage. Dating from 1907, it was one of the oldest structures in town. Surviving both the 1912 and 1936 fires that razed the city, it was a real landmark.

Sadly, this was probably the last year the festival's opening celebration would be held in it, and even that took some arm-twisting with the chief of the fire department. Ole hoped that was why there seemed to be so many cars this year. The parking lot was nearly full. People who thought they might want to leave early, and were afraid of getting boxed in, had parked their cars and trucks all along the shoulder of the road too. "Looks pretty crowded," Sally noted. "Yep," said Ole, worried that the packed house had more to do with the theme this year than it did with sentimental farewells to the rotting hall. Ole and Sally sidled in the front door.

Before others accosted them, the memories came flooding back: the familiar faces, the antique light fixtures with incandescent bulbs scattered around high on the walls, the wooden floor, the waves of food smells coming from the kitchen, the bustle of the band setting up on the stage, and a riot of unsupervised kids running around underfoot. The old hall was made for kids and Sally and Ole had gone through all the adventure phases together as childhood friends.

The grade school kids liked to scamper around in the dust and cobwebs of an attic filled with mysterious objects. Scrambling up and down the old fold-down ladder was half the fun. A few cuts, bruises, spider-bites and sniffles from the dust were attended to each year, but that was just part of the deal.

Pre-teens migrated to the musty, evil-smelling basement lined with dark indentions and crumbling shelves along the walls. Entering through the trapdoor lent its aura of finality to the descent below into the "dungeon." The boys thought they were very savvy luring the girls down there to taunt and scare them with ghost and spook stories about the denizens of the gloomy underbelly of the hall. Really, the rapidly maturing girls just let the boys have that impression so they could steal kisses to brag about to their girlfriends at the next pajama party.

Thinking nobody noticed, teens typically paired off

into couples and furtively snuck into the woods out back or into the old adjoining tool shed for a little more serious hanky panky. Little did they know their parents had done the same thing and were not terribly worried about trouble because they knew there were few comfortable places to get supine, and although the cold and damp elicited a protective hug or two, that only lasted so long before the girls wanted to come back inside.

"So, Ole, ya remember the first time?" Sally teased.

"Huh, wha ..." Ole started. His attention had quickly moved on from the memories to determining who was likely to approach him first about the night on the bog.

"Oh come on, Ole, ya know, the First Time!" she digged.

"Oh, ya mean our first kiss!?" he belatedly caught up.

"What else didja think I meant?" Sally asked with mock exasperation. Ole had been fairly serious as a kid, and a little more shy and reticent than most, so the first time had been under a spruce out back rather than as a trick in the dungeon.

"Oh, I remember it all right," he acknowledged, "and it was real pleasant an' all, but I didn't know you were supposed to use your tongue," he tapered off roguishly.

This time Sally's jab was in his ribs, and a bit less gentle, but it simply elicited an oofing guffaw from Ole. Once again, she had managed to put him at ease when entering a social situation he had approached with some trepidation.

Good thing, too. He saw several members of the Cranberry Farmer's Association (CFA) angling their way through the crowd towards him and the gaggle was clustered on the stairs to the stage whispering and pointing at him. Others in the crowd, mostly the women, were a bit more discreet with their glances. Of course, they might have been noting his date too. All the previous times he had been set up to attend with someone else, the evening had been an embarrassing ordeal. That's why he had stopped doing it years ago. But, what the hey? He'd rather they gossip about him and Sally than about the night in the bog. Sally didn't seem to mind either. She knew the score.

"Hey Ole! Hey Sally!" The first fellow bog farmer to reach him was boisterous Bob Newall from up the road apiece. "Gee it's right fine ta see ya two here together. Whadit take ya ta haul him along Sally?"

"Just a smile and a wink, Bob. How's things?"

" Ya mean my body, my business, my berries, my bogs, or my maiden?" Bob wisecracked with a smirk and a leer that Ole deemed highly inappropriate in mixed company. Here it begins.

"I meant your bod, Bob, but I guess your own private bog maiden can attend to that, eh?"

"I wish! How do you do it Ole?"

"By not digging up every last native bog to plant cranberries, Bob!" Ole retorted with more vehemence than he intended. That took Bob aback, but it shut him up too. For a few moments anyway, and now the topic was changed.

"What's gotten inta ya Ole? I thought you was a gung-ho cranberry farmer. Not like you don't control half the market on the West Coast. Why're ya givin' me grief about planting some more fields? Are ya still on board with the project plans?"

Ole just grumbled a noncommittal mumble and avoided Bob's distressed and quizzical expression by staring around the room for someplace else to be.

If Maybelle's tales about the night on the bog were the only rumor Ole had to contend with, matters would be easier, if still unpleasant. However, Bugsy, as president of the CFA, had also intimated at the last board meeting (Ole hadn't attended) that Ole seemed to be having second thoughts about the Joint Cranberry Bogs Expansion Project, or JCBEP for short. (Nobody could think of a catchy acronym, so they just abbreviated the logical name.) The JCBEP was the biggest undertaking in the history of the CFA, and they needed all the farmers on board, even those not directly affected by the plan, to sell it to the county and state regulators. Market demand for cranberries continued to increase, but enough production was coming online in Washington State, the upper Midwest, the Northeast, and Canada, that prices remained depressed and profit margins were slim. All the local land that was easily converted to cranberry bogs already had been. Transforming new areas from native bogs to cranberry farms was going to entail sophisticated modifications to natural drainage patterns and expensive pumping and irrigation facilities. The only way the farmers thought they could profitably pull off the expanded commodity production to capture newly emerging market share was by collaborating on a joint development project. Ole's farmland and cooperation were central to the project in terms of strategic acreage, drainage, financing and political support. The association had been planning this for years and had already spent a bundle on lawyer's fees to start submitting the required permit applications with the county and state land use boards, water regulatory agencies, wildlife agencies and what-not. Bugsy had all the CFA members a-jitter with what he had said about Ole at the last meeting, and more than one of them wanted to find out in person tonight what he was thinking.

Before Ole could escape Bob, he was cornered by Jake Booley whose base of operations consisted of scattered cranberry bogs to the southeast of Ole's farm.

"Hey Sally! Hey Ole!" Jake greeted them, Sally first, as was more respectful, Ole thought.

Then Jake caught the puzzlement on Bob's face and injected, "What's up?"

"Everything that's not down." Ole evaded.

"Ole's getting on my case about planting more bogs. Go figure." Bob vented towards Ole but in response to Jake's question.

"That so, Ole?" asked Jake cautiously.

"I just said we shouldn't be converting every last natural bog, that's all." Ole defended himself.

Jake eyed his neighbor with concern and was about to ask for further clarification when Ole was saved by the evening's host taking the microphone to begin the festivities. Sally excused them and led Ole to a back table, off to the side, but perfectly situated near the sole restroom and the back door.

The evening proceeded pretty much as Ole had expected. The emcee rattled off his interminable list of announcements, thanks, news bits, and personal observations about the importance and history of the festival. Matronly farmers' wives and their conscripted daughters (and even a few disgruntled sons) bustled back and forth between the kitchen and the tables with serving platters full of victuals fit for a king. This was no common American feed; they lived on the Oregon coast! Even if the offerings were a bit mismatched, who cared? They might not be big city sophisticates, pairing this with that, but they knew good food when they tasted it, and they simply served the incredible abundance that was locally available.

Fresh seafood topped the fare. Members of the Confederated Tribes of the Sand Coast had set up a grill out back of the hall (further frustrating young couples) and had lightly seared half a dozen freshly caught Coho salmon on cedar planks immediately before the feast began. Families engaged in commercial seafood production provided succulent flounder, snapper, shrimp, crabs, oysters, clams, and mussels on mixed platters and in stews. One fisherman, who had spent some time off the coast of California that summer, had traded some of his catch for the carcasses of several wild boars that he then donated to the festival. Another wild-crafter had some butter infused with the aroma of native Oregon truffles that he had collected last winter in the foothills of the Umpqua Valley. Patties of the truffle butter where spotted on the hot sliced boar meat to melt and create a taste sensation too good for a king, although it actually elicited exclamations ranging from disgust to uncertainty to ecstasy among diners unfamiliar with the olfactory sensation. A local logger had been stocking his freezer with grouse he had been plunking all summer long on the job. His wife glazed the birds with a sweet-spicy hazelnut sauce. One inland relative of a cranberry farmer brought a wild turkey, redolent with acorn-flavored dark meat.

To complement the main courses, there were mounds of garlic-flavored mashed potatoes, bowls of wild rice, fresh baked home-made rolls, chanterelle mushroom gravy, fried slices of local king bolete mushrooms, corn on the cob, summer squash camouflaged in a variety of breads and vegie casseroles, salad trays with fresh garden produce. Local farmers provided an assortment of handcrafted cheeses, cream cheese dips and ice creams. And, there were more wild-berry pies than you could shake a fork at! World-class wines from the Willamette, Umpqua, and Rogue Valleys accompanied the extravagant victuals as well as lager, ale and stout beers from nearby microbreweries. Of course, the best cranberry sauce in the world graced every plate.

A buffet style serving line might have been easier, but there was not enough of any one dish to go around and not enough room to lay it all out on separate tables. Certain individuals were targeted with special menu items, but for almost everyone, what was placed on your table constituted the fixin's for a sumptuous lottery meal. Many dietary constraints were suspended for the evening and diners engaged in lively barter for tastes or servings of personally craved foods. Each table had a tall stack of small clean plates for just such swapping. Even the servers seemed to enjoy all the bustling, confusion, and noise. The clamorous chaos also made it easier to tune out the emcee until the fun events began.

When the crowd began to seriously chow down, and quiet down, the real entertainment ensued on stage. There was the Best Berries Contest, the Cranberry Haiku Poetry

Contest, and the Cranberry Farmer Fashion Show, all conducted with way tongue-in-cheek seriousness that elicited roars of self-deprecating laughter and waves of applause from the gorging audience. Finally, as the food intake slowed, there came the coronation of the Berry Queen, the event Ole had particularly been dreading because it gave Maybelle the chance to mouth off at length about how she had selected this year's theme. The line to the sole restroom had shortened as people ate and Ole moved to go stand in cue, but Sally would have nothing of it and grabbed his arm, sitting him back down.

"No you don't Ole, you're not leaving me alone to be stared at. We can talk about it all you want afterwards if you like, but you are sitting here next to me for the coronation, even if you wet your pants!"

Ole didn't like the sound of that, but fortunately, his bladder wasn't really that full and he could see Sally's point. "OK," and he meekly sat down.

The emcee had called the Berry Theme Committee (they also doubled as the Coronation Committee) up on stage for the event of the evening. More conscripted young lads were now clearing the tables in preparation for moving them to clear a dance floor.

"And NOW! Ladies and Gentlemen!" Blah, blah, blah, yadda, yadda, yadda he droned on. The slightly pudgy Maybelle sat fidgeting on the Berry Throne in her gray silky dress with lichens draped on her shoulders, trying valiantly to look alluring and to maintain her forced smile indefinitely and unwaveringly. If she was supposed to represent a bog maiden apparition, she had succeeded.

Finally, Bugs, in his dual role as head of the

Coronation Committee and president of the CFA, approached Maybelle with the Berry Crown. Tacky was one word to describe it, but it had been made long ago and was traditional. Maybelle fidgeted even more because she knew she would finally get to speak.

No sooner had Bugsy lowered the crown and voiced the old All hail ye the Berry Queen accolade, than Maybelle was on her feet and jabbering away. The emcee had not even had the opportunity to ask her to bestow her "berry astute wisdom" on the gathered multitudes. Just as well, it was a horrible pun, proclaimed annually in an agonizing cycle of groaning reiteration.

Maybelle was just getting warmed up with her tale about her inspiration for this year's theme by describing how she and her friends had followed some boy into the bogs on Ole's farm.

That was that! Ole could take no more. He bolted to his feet with a booming, "Oh yeah!? So you are now telling us all how you and your friends decided to trespass on my property!?"

Maybe not a pin—there was still some clanking in the kitchen—but anyone with average hearing or a turned-up hearing aid could have certainly heard a pencil drop. A sea of stunned faces swiveled to Ole. Maybelle seemed to be choking on the microphone. The gaggle of high school girls on the stage stairs inhaled simultaneously and held their breaths. Sheriff Ray, sitting in the corner, held his head bent down over his empty plate and was just slowly shaking it back and forth. Sally's eyes were examining the upper inside of her skull. Bugs had spun a circle on the stage and slapped his thigh as he struggled to suppress an outburst of uncontrollable hooting. The emcee slowly drifted off stage, as in a trance. The Coronation Committee apparently thought their shoes worthy of close examination.

You had to hand it to the Boggy Bottom Boys band; they knew a cue when they saw one. Without missing a fore beat, they broke into their first song of the evening and the tableau was shattered, actually, to the relief of almost everyone. Fortunately they had prepped for a smooth and rapid transition from the coronation to boogie-down dancing by setting up behind the throne and being ready to bust into music as soon as Maybelle finished her oration. Even the band seemed pleased for an excuse to start preemptively. Maybelle looked confused and distraught, but Sheriff Ray was certainly relieved.

Ole sat back down. Sally lowered her eyes, put her arm around Ole's shoulders, and released a sigh as she slumped against him. People stood and stretched, the line to the sole restroom grew (funny how it was mostly women), tables were moved aside, and some of the younger folk who hadn't eaten too much started dancing.

"Come on Ole, I don't know how much longer I can keep you here, but I simply must have one dance with you."

What had gotten in to him, Ole thought? He had never made a scene like that before. Yet again, Sally had come to the rescue, offering him a way to ease back into the scene rather than sneaking out of the hall in shame. Actually, he did want to dance with Sally. She just looked so darn, well, alluring! Shapely, well-attired, perfect posture, confident moves.

"Whew! I didn't know you could dance so hot, Sal," he

puffed after several fast numbers.

"Yeah, I guess that was one thing I learned from my hyperactive ex. He just always had to be doing something, and more often than not he drug me out dancing, so to speak."

"You're gonna have to teach me Sally, you have a lot more moves than little ol' me."

"First of all, you ain't so little Ole, and secondly, I could give a hoot about moves … at least on the dance floor," she said a bit seductively.

Just then, both of them espied Stan Latterly getting up from his chair across the room and noticed he seemed to be circling towards them.

"Come on Ole, here comes that money grubbing greed-head of a real estate agent. Let's skeedadle. I did want to dance some slow ones with you tonight, but the band never gets around to chest-huggers till the third set."

Ole shrugged. "Right you are, on all accounts, but I have a Victrola and some hefty 78s back at my humble abode. Care to come over for some schmaltzy music?"

Sally broke into an expansive grin, took his arm and dragged him out of the hall. Ole thought he could hear her purring, nestled under his arm in the cab of the pickup, all the way back to his house.

∫

"Humble abode?" Sally asked with an accent on the first word. "I thought you still lived in your folks'es house." Even in the dark it was obvious they were approaching the family property through a newly landscaped entrance. At least, it was new to Sally.

"Nah, my assistants and their family live in the old place now."

"Assistants? You mean farm employees?"

"No, well, not entirely. Gabriela and Hector Hernandez and their kids. She takes care of my household affairs, and he supervises work around the farm."

"House attendant!? Fulltime farm supervisor?" Sally was astonished. Doubly so when they rounded a curve in the driveway and the truck's headlamps illuminated a close-up view of the new house. "McMansion" was the first word that came to Sally's mind, but she quickly revised her impression as they got out and approached.

For starters, it wasn't huge, just new. Unlike other such housing anomalies that provided a faux sense of place to the transplanted nouveau riche, this dwelling seemed to fit very naturally into the surrounding landscape. Simple low lines, local rock and wood exterior, and tasteful, low-maintenance landscaping. Her impression was that of a cross between modern rural comfort and Japanese simplicity.

"Been doin' OK by yourself, eh Ole?" she squeezed his arm.

"Yep, business has been pretty good," he understated. Ole was by nature modest, but he couldn't help noticing that Sally was impressed, so he continued. "The old family residence was just too much upkeep, or rather, I didn't want to do the repairs myself anymore, I wanted to concentrate on the cranberries. Besides, after dad died, I just decided I didn't need daily reminders of the months I spent at his beside as he wasted away."

"Sorry." Sally said simply. Her mom had kept her informed of Bert's long struggle with cancer, but she had not been able to attend the funeral because her husband had insisted on climbing a peak in the North Cascades National Park that weekend.

"Anyway," Ole justified, "new houses are a good investment and a tax write-off, so I figured I might as well live comfortably."

"Well," Sally said semi-sarcastically (toward herself really), "so much for my vision of your bachelor pad."

Inside, Sally's appreciation of his house became more nuanced. Not too big, but plenty of room for comfort, and outfitted with the most up-to-date energy efficiencies, amenities and appliances. All very tastefully done too.

"Eschewing ostentatiousness," her ex would have declared, showing off his vocabulary.

Sally just squeezed Ole's arm again and said sincerely, "I really like it Ole."

Kicking off their shoes in the mudroom entrance to the kitchen, Ole brought up some lights around the house, but just some, and just somewhat.

"Make yourself at home. There's some good wine in the cabinet next to the fridge. I'll be right back."

When Ole returned, Sally had three different bottles of Oregon Pinot Noir sitting on the counter. She was scratching her head, trying to decide among them.

"Free loadin' skateboarders, Ole, I thought you were a country hick! At least you were when we were kids."

"You too Sally, you have certainly changed a fair schmidgen."

"Well, you still talk like a hick, but where did you get

your taste in wines? Did you buy it?" Sally joked, belatedly hoping Ole knew it was only a joke.

Unfazed, Ole filled in some more details of his life since she had been gone. Old high school buddy starting a vineyard in the valley, meeting him at an agricultural trade association meeting, follow-up reciprocal visits at the winery and the cranberry farm, swapped cranberry cultivation and oenological lessons, that sort of thing. Nothing fancy, just enjoying good Oregon wine.

"I dusted off the old Victrola. Want me to crank it up?"

"No! I thought you were just joking, Ole. That old antique of your folks still works!?"

"Yep, Ma and Pa took real good care of it. Of their 78s too. You remember how picky they were about supervision when we wanted to play with it as kids."

Of course, I just didn't think it could have actually survived us in working condition."

"Want to dance one of those slow dances, Sally?"

"I would never pass up a 78 RPM chest-hugger with a Norwegian bachelor farmer, Ole."

Now they were both smiling real big. An outside observer would have sworn their faces were a little flushed too. There might have been a hint of pheromones in the air.

∫

Ole wasn't a virgin, but he wasn't exactly experienced either. His few sexual encounters had ranged from vaguely remembered (drunk) through unrewarding (frigid partner) and embarrassing (lack of performance on his part) to shameful (lying). The one time he thought he was truly in love (the romantic variety), he had unabashedly worshipped his partner. He put her on a pedestal of perfection and his desire could see no faults in her. Which wasn't exactly fair to her, either. He was disabused of his notions before too long, and even though she had tried to let him down softly, it was still a crash and burn landing. Ole had long since stopped trying. Few people asked him about his love life anymore and Ole didn't bring the topic up. Bonny was the only person who was still really trying to hitch her gentle friend up with a good gal.

In any case, this was different. How could I ever have known it could be so good? Ole asked himself. The clock on the bed stand read 7:45 and the day was way past dawning outside. Normally, Ole would have been out and about for an hour now, dealing with farm chores. Heck, he reflected, life is nothing but a collection of a long series of moments, and if you don't appreciate them along the way, then your collection is kinda tawdry. Anyway, he was darn tootin' sure not going to miss appreciating this series of moments. Thank goodness Hector was so responsible and reliable.

While he had considered Sally self-assured, stylish, friendly, and supportive the night before, the only word that came to mind now was voluptuous. Never in his most feverish teenage fantasy could he have imagined that a full-grown mature woman could feel so good lying naked next to him in the morning, softly slumbering. As for the culmination of the night before, well, it was going to take a long time for him to process that. Maybe repetition would help?

"Mmpphmmphf ... aaahhh, mmm ... Oooollee" Sally
muffled into his chest hairs as she roused to semi-conscious
sensuousness with little kisses to his skin as she snuggled
even closer, if that was possible.

OK, so not all moments in your life's collection are
equal, Ole decided as he arched his back and started
stretching his numb arm in response to Sally's half-dream
ministrations. If it was pheromones during the dance last
night, it was slumberomones this morning. Sally also
stretched, mumbled some more ardent nothings, and slowly
slid on top of Ole again, drowning him in the wonder of
her perfectly proportioned breasts, hips and thighs. Half in
a trance, half in the crystal clear light of the low angled
morning sun streaming through the windows, they made
love again. Slowly, softly, intensely.

"Sally, I never could have imagined ..."

"Don't! Please, Ole, just don't say it. Not yet anyway.
Let's just let it sink in. We are sharing this moment. We
know what it means. Just let it settle, OK?" she pleaded
gently.

"You're right Sal, I don't know what's gotten into me.
I usually don't talk so much."

Go figure, Sally thought. It was obvious that Ole's
thoughts were ripe for plucking. Sally hadn't really planned
it that way, but she knew an opportunity when she saw one.
A little nudging here, a gentle query there.

"It's just, well, ever since ..." A long pause of silence
ensued.

"Ever since what, Ole?" she prompted.

"Well, you know, that bog thing."

"Hold that thought, Ole."

This might take a little while, Sally guessed. Quick trips to the bathroom and grabbing coffee they smelled brewing in the timed percolator delayed any immediate reasons for getting out of bed, once they had jumped back in. It was Saturday morning after all, and Ole had turned his ear crab off after calling Hector to discuss pressing chores around the farm that morning.

"Now, that bog thing. Ole, I don't want to press you, but if you want someone to talk to about the incident, you know I won't make like Maybelle or Bugsy."

Ole looked at her with trust and relief, and he knew she was simply stating the truth. It seemed almost as if she really wanted to just share his burden and, with her nestled next to him, he came to the retrospectively obvious realization that he really wanted to talk to someone about it.

After describing how he had followed the trespassing Johnny Wanders across his farm berms to the haunted Old Grove Bog, and how he was in turn followed by the gaggle, and how he had chased befuddled Johnny out of the Old Grove to the hysteria and astonishment of the giggling gaggle, Ole got to the crux of the matter.

"It was past dusk, but not completely dark. That time when the colors have faded, but your black and white vision is doing as good as in full moonlight. When I confronted him, Johnny crashed off into the bushes and then I heard him go thunk, like a wet mattress dropped from a pickup bed onto a mud flat. Cripes, I thought, liability up the wazoo here! Just then, in the corner of my eye, I caught this translucent figure floating out over the bog. The giggling of the gaggle seemed to fade into the distance, as if the sound lost substance. Everything else seemed to wash out too. Not just like it was still getting darker, it was like, I don't know, like turning down the contrast knob on an old black and white TV I guess. Then ..." Ole paused again.

Sally pressed closer for encouragement, but didn't try to be sexy; she was just letting him know she was listening.

After a few moments, Ole continued. "Well, I didn't think I would admit it, but those giggling high school girls didn't do so bad portraying her on the banner."

Her, Sally thought. This was the first time Ole had ever admitted seeing the female apparition of rumor. Maybe some of the gaggle had really seen it too?

"She was all mist and fog and insubstantial, yet her form undulated slowly, kinda sultry-like; I couldn't take my eyes off of her, there—floating out there—rising up out of the water in the middle of the bog." Ole cringed a bit and covered his eyes as if struggling with the elusive memory in the light of waxing day.

"That's when I heard her, but not speaking really. She wasn't actually talking to me. It was more like I felt her intent deep inside. More like beseeching or spellbinding. Drawing me to her with her deep, deep desire. Not sexual mind you!" Ole quickly added.

Sally avoided looking at him or saying anything, but just murmured, "Go on."

"It was almost like she wanted my mind for something and was examining it. Like there were tendrils between our minds and she was slowing pulling me to her. Tempting me with a union of souls. Luring me in with her desperate need. Enticing me with her sensuality to capture my mind and ..." Ole caught himself up short.

He had said enough, more than enough. What was he thinking? Did he want to blow a perfect night and morning? Even a gal as open and understanding as Sally must be wondering about his sanity and desires about now. Indeed, Sally seemed pensive as they busied themselves with breakfast and Ole drove her home.

"Sal, I don't know what to say. That was the best time I have had in a long time. Please don't read too much into the bog maiden thing. I was just imagining things."

"Ole, you big huggable bear of a man, you had best call me soon, or I'll have my mom sic Bonny on you again."

Still, Ole understood he had said too much. Whoever believed that being taciturn was maladaptive? The crows in Holly's yard, however, were not bashful about expressing their opinions, verbally or otherwise.

Chapter 2 — Vision Quest

ear my prayer.
I honor the Great Mystery
I honor all that is
I honor our home on Mother Earth
I honor the many beings sharing this home
I honor my ancestors
I honor my fellow travelers
I honor myself
I honor my experience
Hear my intent
I offer my tale
Grant me my name
Show me my path
That my honor may be strong
Hear my tale.

I am called Johnny Wanders, but that is not my real name. I do not have a real name. I seek my real name and my path in life. This is the tale of my lost heritage and my efforts to seek my vision, to learn my life's meaning, to gather my power, to find my helpers, so that I can act properly in this world. I offer you this tale, Great Spirit, Great Mystery. Guide me to the fulfillment of my quest.

My blood is indigenous American. My ancestors long lived here, in the hills, near the sand coast. That is about all I know. My mom and I moved back here from the Siletz Indian Reservation when I was about 5 years old. I never knew my dad and my mom would not talk about him. She was hopeless too. Drunk. Depressed. Jobless. Lost. We lived in squalor, although at the time, it was all I knew.

When I was about 10, my aunt Jenny started taking care of me. At least someone cooked meals for me again, and my bedding and clothes were clean, but Aunt Jenny's skinny live-in boyfriend Jack was a royal pain in the butt. Also jobless, into drugs and drinking, he often beat Jenny and seemed to get a kick out of scaring and intimidating me. He thought I was his little slave.

"Get me another beer you lazy Indian," or "Get lost, your aunt and I have business to attend to," he would bellow.

At least I was getting big and angry enough that after a few scraps he didn't try to slap me around anymore. I just figured Aunt Jenny made her own choices. The local police and Oregon State Social Services intervened several times, but Jenny and Jack acted sorry for a while and the public agency budgets were such that I was soon back in the same domestic situation.

When I was fourteen, I ran away from home, but didn't get very far. Upon being returned, I was housed with a white family who took in troubled youth. Faye and Bill. They were decent, well meaning folk, but by then I was well on the path to being a rebellious and disrespectful teen. I became a hippy. I thought that growing my hair long and trying various drugs would somehow connect me with my

Indian heritage. Except for a small circle of drug-using friends, I was scorned by most of the kids at high school as that "hippy Indian kid" or HIK for short, so I withdrew from many social activities and became somewhat of a loner. I wasn't dumb or ignorant though. When I couldn't get out of the house in mid-winter I would hole up in my room with books on philosophy, comparative religions, new age metaphysics, science fiction, or historical fiction. If some topic caught my fancy, I often wandered down long roads of discovery. However, I most definitely did not like being told what to study, so my grades suffered.

The one excellent period of my youth was the last year in high school when I hung out with Grace Flores for a while. She was so righteous! Pretty, affectionate, funny, lively, and bright. Every time I was around her, it seemed like there was a spot of sunlight slicing through the threatening clouds of my life, shinning right on us. I was stupid enough not to appreciate what our budding relationship could have meant. She loved me, I could tell, but she needed me to straighten up for her. Instead, I clung to my pain, self-pity, and drugs.

When Grace left for college, she said things like, "I can't stay here Johnny, the world is just too full of possibilities," or "I have to follow my path, Johnny, I need to find out what I can become."

What I heard was, "I don't want you anymore Johnny." "You're not good enough for me." "Forget about us, so I don't have to feel guilty about leaving you."

I couldn't pay for college or get accepted anyway, even if I had wanted to attend. I was devastated and sank deeper into my despair and drifting.

Soon I ended up spending a few months in the county jail for petty theft. Boring! Reading was about all I had to pass the time and distract myself from my tedious circumstances. One day, Mary Duneflower Jackson, a tribal elder who owns a local bookstore, visited me. Although I didn't know Mary well, she knew my mom, Aunt Jenny, and the sad saga of my upbringing. She didn't say much during her visit, at least not verbally. Maybe "Hey Johnny," but her eyes spoke volumes. She gave me some books on Native American cultures. "Here."

I devoured them. She came again, and gave me some more on Native American spirituality. "Maybe these too." She never preached. She never exhorted me to do or be anything, unlike so many of my former arrogant caregivers and teachers. She knew I was a captive audience and, I think, understood my need. What I read about the notion of vision quests struck a chord in my being that resonated like a gong. I knew I had to find my path. I knew I had to find myself. At that time, I only knew I had to do this or self-destruct. Later I learned that I had to do this because I owed it to all creation for the privilege of my life.

When I got out of the clink, I asked around about how to undertake a vision quest. My few inquiries with tribal members about what that might entail were met with howls of laughter, ridicule, blank looks of incomprehension, or shrugs of disinterest. I was afraid to ask the people who might really know: elders like Mary Duneflower or Wally One-Path Jackson, who was Mary's nephew and tribal head. These stern and serious council members just seemed too imposing to me. They might want to start dictating my life again. Or even worse, what if they laughed at my ideas. I wanted to do this on my own, by myself.

So I just made it up from what I had read and what little I knew about our tribe. I had found historical records of the two original tribal clans; those who lived on the dunes and those who inhabited the inland hills. Although considered the same "Indians" by white colonists, the cultures differed. When I was a kid, mom had only once mentioned my ancestry.

One night in a fit of drunken pride she proclaimed boastfully and sarcastically, "You were born to the mighty descendants of the ... Mishikte ... the Mitishwutme ... the ... hills clan! ... of the local Apathaskan tribe of southwestern Oregon!" Then back to the wine bottle and TV.

Not only couldn't she remember the name of our band, but she had mispronounced the name for our language group (it is spelled "Athapaskan." Apath(y) indeed!). My jailhouse reading had revealed that the Athapaskan language group included a variety of Native American Nations (called "First Peoples" in Canada) that ranged discontinuously from Alaska to the deserts of the American Southwest. Such a broad grouping explained little about our tribe.

After disease, land theft, war, and forcible relocation to the Siletz Reservation to the north, there remained few descendants of the original inhabitants of the local area. When Mom and I moved back to the south coast a couple of decades ago, the hill and dune clans had been combined to form the Confederated Tribes of the Sand Coast. They had done so in order to secure federal recognition, obtain a measly payoff, and get back a little bit of the seemingly worthless land on the boggy dunes. Most of the upland hills that my own tribe originally inhabited were now covered with private ranches, sprawling ranchette housing developments, and corporate timberlands. The confederated tribes no longer held title to any of it. The small patches of county, state, and federal forestlands in the foothills were often inundated with tourists and campers seeking solace from their fancy homes and parking lot covered towns, so I didn't want to try my vision quest there.

Instead of heading for my clan's hills, I decided to pursue my vision quest on the dunes near the sea. Near the Wayward River I knew of an area where a person could lose oneself in miles of dense pine forests and shrub lands between the ocean and inland cranberry farms. It is part of our now-combined confederated tribal land and that is where I headed. From what I read of vision quests, I knew they often involved ritual prayers coupled with fasting, sleeplessness, and extreme exertion to induce altered states of consciousness. I hadn't inherited any specific prayers, so I made up my own. I was tempted to take drugs and short-circuit the vision process, but in the end, I just walked out there and gave it a go. I took only the clothes I was wearing and a lighter so I could start a fire if I needed the warmth. It was May. Not extreme weather on the coast, but not warm either.

I started a fire the first night and collected some leaves of aromatic shrubs for a smoke-cleansing ritual. That was fun. Staying awake that night seemed brave, but come morning, my stomach was growling, and I was having second thoughts. I stuck with it though. That day I walked for miles through the forest until it got dark. At one point I was far inland and was winding my way through swampy areas with bizarre vegetation. I came upon an especially contorted and stunted grove of very old oak trees next to a bog. The place positively oozed weirdness. I felt a sort of premonition that scared me, so I retreated and walked back towards the sea. I had to keep moving to stay awake that night. I climbed and rolled down sand dunes. I swam across the chilly Wayward River and walked miles up and down the beach weaving among flashes of brilliant moonlight that jabbed through gaps in the racing clouds. I chased gulls and imaginary creatures. The waves glowed a luminescent green as they crashed and with each step I took on the wet sand, rays of green fluorescence would stab out in starburst patterns around my foot.

Shortly after dawn I collapsed in a hollow, sheltered by tall beach grass, and slept like a beached driftwood log. Only as I eventually stirred in the deepening dusk and cold wind of an approaching storm—in that realm between sleep and awakening, dream and reality—did my mind give me a minor vision, the hint I needed to continue on my path. I was in that ominous grove of twisted and contorted oak trees again, on the edges of the bog. This time, the forest floor was not bare. Magnificent huge red mushrooms with bright yellowish-white dots on their caps and yellow stems carpeted the grove, right up to the edge of the bog. The contrast between the dazzling mushrooms and the gloomy surroundings was uncanny. I felt like I was in an alternate reality, in a primeval place, with ancient beings watching me, gazing achingly at me. Then a raven cawed abruptly as it flew directly over my head and I awoke startled and disoriented.

I couldn't exactly call it a successful vision quest. I had not attained my path, my purpose, or my identity, as I had sought. All I had really done was stumble around the dunes for a few days without food or sleep. Who would consider the strange mushrooms I saw in my dream as spirit helpers? A bear, a cougar, an eagle, or a whale; now any of those would be worthy totems. Nevertheless, as I recovered I felt as if I had taken the first step. The dream seemed significant.

$$\int$$

In the coming weeks, I figured out where the grove of oaks was located. The city librarian greeted me with disbelief.

"Johnny, What are you doing here!?"

I ignored his derision and logged onto the public use computers. With Google Earth, I examined the area where I had done my vision quest. The resolution was low along this remote stretch of the Oregon Coast, but I got a general idea of where I had been. Next, I went to the county records office and got maps of land ownership.

"Johnny! What a surprise ... you want what?" and "Hmmph, you planning on buying some bogs?"

The bog bordered by the grove of oaks appeared to be on property owned by a cranberry farmer named Ole Gorseman. Acres of his rectangular cranberry bogs lay just beyond the trees that surrounded the natural bog; I had wandered off the tribal lands a little bit. I knew who Ole was, but had never met him.

The librarian reluctantly let me check out books on

mushrooms. It seems he was a member of the South Coast Mushroom Club and took a skeptical interest in why I wanted to know about mushrooms.

"You're not trying to find information on those recreational mushrooms?" he asked, no doubt suspecting so from my reputation.

I already knew all about the blue-staining silver ladies and had often seen the red-with-white-spots amanitas in the nearby forests. I had never eaten any of the amanitas though, because they were huge and I disliked the taste of raw mushrooms. Besides which, several of my friends had tried them and the experience they described was not very tempting.

The ones in my dream were distinctly different anyway. Both the spots on the cap and the entire stem were definitely yellow, not white.

"Nope," the librarian responded, "there aren't any such species of *Amanita* mushrooms. Anyway, they are all poisonous. I recommend you just stay away from them all!"

With his judgmental blanket statements, he sounded about as knowledgeable as my grade school teacher or the editor for the local newspaper, so I mostly ignored him. He was right about one thing; the red one with white spots, *Amanita muscaria*, was the closest match I could find. With a bit more delving, I found more about how this mushroom had a long history in Europe, Russia, and Asia as an entheogen and spirit guide for shamans. One authority even speculated that this species of mushroom was the "Soma" praised in the ancient Vedic hymns of India and he called it the "Divine Mushroom of Immortality." In spite of their uncertain identity, I felt increasingly sure that the mushrooms of my dream were meant to be the next guides in my spirit quest. I was reluctant to try any drug again, especially ones my friends had dissed so badly, but I also strongly felt that dream omens were probably ignored at one's peril, or at least, great loss.

In early August, I decided I needed to find out. I felt restless and driven; not like any doom was descending on me, but more like my path was outlined in neon lights that formed big pointy arrows. In a moment of unrestrained enthusiasm, I confided my plans to a younger friend that I trusted. That was a big mistake.

"Don't you dare say a word!" I had pleaded.

"I won't, Johnny! Oh Gawd, that is sooo cool, I just, like, wish I could, like, watch!"

Well, she blabbed. A callous clique of teeny-bopping female thrill-seekers followed me, not to mention Ole. I found out what happened later, although I experienced the immediate and riveting repercussions that night.

There had been an early August rainstorm several days earlier and some mushrooms were beginning to sprout. I selected a quickly darkening cloudy day to sneak through Ole's farm around dusk. To come in from the dunes would have involved many miles of additional hiking through brush lands that I had only explored during my vision quest. The waning quarter moon was bright enough behind the clouds so I could find my way in the growing gloom. As I approached the bog and oak grove, I got a tingling feeling in my spine, like something potent was about to happen, but I was not about to quit now. I slowly entered the grove. I walked very carefully, looking for the mushrooms of my dream. There they were! Their colors were washed out in the fading light, but something about the dots on their caps suggested to me that they might be the right ones. Flicking my lighter on briefly, I confirmed the dots on the caps had a light yellowish tint and the stems were yellow too, just like in my dream, not the books.

I sat down in a circle of them. Unnerving as the whole scene was, this felt right. A shiver of anticipation ascended my spine. This was my next step to self-discovery. They were almost calling to me or enticing me somehow. It was sort of like the mushrooms in Alice in Wonderland saying, "Please eat me, please eat me" or some such. I dismissed the silly white culture fantasies and after I recited some of my made-up prayers, I ate a big one that was right in front of me. It tasted, well, like a raw mushroom. It was not easy to eat the whole thing. Suppressing my gag reflex, I choked it down as quickly as I could, chewing as little as possible. Then I simply sat and waited for whatever came next. Calm owl hoots. Silence. Perturbed owl hoots. Time passed and it got darker. Then I saw some dim lights flickering between trees across the bog, heard some twigs snapping and caught faint broken snatches of girly whispers. Still, I did not comprehend that I had been followed. I paid little heed as these vague and distant clues faded.

I sat quietly for a while longer. Then what happened next is very hard to describe. One moment I was in this world, and the next I was in another. No transition. First, I was just sitting in a strange grove and then I found myself a passenger in a luminous, vibrating, confined bulb of reality that was only as wide as the bog and grove. The immediate realm that I could perceive was the whole of my world, but it was far more poignant, significant, and alive than anything I had ever experienced before. Nothing was distorted, but every minutia of my surroundings was infused with a sense of supreme importance. I felt I could simultaneously embrace every radiating detail of this narrow world. As I noted these strange sensations, I started to sweat and feel feverish. It was getting harder to focus on any one thing, although I felt like I could share the inner being of all the creatures immediately around me: the trees, the moss, the insects, the birds, and especially the mushrooms. Suddenly, there was something else—someone else—two other entities! They seemed to stare into my mind and I felt an intense craving emanate from them. I shrank in fear from their presence. My head swam. I got dizzy and must have slumped to the ground. My mind swirled in and out of lucidity. It shifted from this realm to another and back. Then I heard the most unexpected sound.

It was giggling. No, it was the cackling of a gaggle of geese. No, it was the muffled snickering and yakking of teenaged girls. It was the twittering of bushtits. It was the incessant buzz of crickets. I stopped caring as I slipped into a whirling daze and became nauseous with the spinning.

In spite of my confusion and stupor, I did not mistake the blast of the shotgun fired at close range. The sound felt like twin wrecking balls simultaneously slamming both sides of my head. The cackling crickets abruptly ceased their buzzing twitters in the reverberating aftermath. I bolted to my feet and another wave of disorientation washed over me. I heard high-pitched screaming, urgent confused babbling, and crashing bushes on the far side of the bog. The shotgun blast had been much closer, though. I knew it in my gut.

That was the instant that the Gorseman Monster shambled into the grove shouting curses and threats at the top of its lungs. On one level I knew it was Ole, but on another level, the demon that swaggered toward me could not have been more frightening if I had encountered a crazed Sasquatch. His face was a wet lurid red. Veins in his neck stuck out like marine hemp rope. His hair was a bristling crown of gorse spines. His eyes glowed demonically and he had fangs instead of teeth.

He was waving his arms and shotgun and, towering over me as he approached, he shrieked "CHRASHIASH GRAGGA KAAPISCH URREEEMA BRACKK PAZKAT KRILLIBGINK" or some such twisted curse.

I turned and ran for my life and immediately crashed headlong into dense brush. Horrified and in shock, I kept trying to scramble away. Blind and befuddled, I was slapped and scrapped and stabbed and tangled and tripped by branches that deliberately grabbed me. Terror drove me on as the lumbering Gorse Demon bore down on me, screeching ever louder and flinging its venom at me. The next thing I knew, I felt a hard sucking thump along my whole body and found I was face down in muck, my right eye buried along with that side of my face.

At the same moment, as far as I could tell, the Gory Fiend stopped shouting and chasing me, and everything became suddenly quiet. I tentatively opened my left eye and with swirling half-vision found myself on the very edge of the bog. Water oozed through the moss mere inches away and as my focus lengthened and I gazed out over the center of the bog, it seemed as if a thick clump of mist was rising up out of the water there, slowly assuming some form.

The outer world swam away again. The inside of my head rotted and my skull sprouted thick shelves with fingers dangling underneath. My toes became roots and these in turn sprouted a fuzz of fine threads. The dangling fingers pointed further and further back in time. The connection between my self and my body loosened. My identity followed the pointing fingers to fade into the depths of countless millennia. My soul started oozing down my roots and then out the delicate web of threads around them. Then one of the mysterious "others" that I had earlier fled loomed near again. He (yes! he) longed for my body, but seemed to hold back. Radiating from him I felt waves of shame, deep duty, ancient longings, dark tragedies, curses, and unforgiven wrongs.

Then, in an instant, this presence withdrew and I awoke to new delusions. I opened my unburied eye and could not believe what it saw. I struggled to lift my head out of the slime and wash off my other eye. Two was no better than one. There in the middle of the bog was the most convincing hallucination I had ever experienced. Floating over the bog was a ghost, a spirit, whatever. It was a woman. She was clothed in mists and wisps of fog, but just barely. Her form was unmistakably full and sensuous. Later thinking of words to describe her, I would say she exuded bottomless desire and a sultry magnetism as she reached out to beckon to me. It took a moment to realize she was not reaching towards me, but off to one side of me a little. That is when my sanity really fled. I swear I saw the Ole Ogre floating out over the water of the bog towards her, an arm outstretched to her in his trance, lost in her spell. They came together, floating over the water in the center of the bog, and embraced. They slowly began to spin in an otherworldly dance and their forms seemed to enfold. It gradually became harder and harder to distinguish where the ghostly maiden left off and the Ole Thing remained.

"GAsp! SKreeech! NO way! WAY! Get outa my Way!" echoed back and forth across the bog.

Then there was a loud "KerPLUNK-Splash" in the middle of the bog like someone doing a cannonball off the high dive. I surrendered my senses and spiraled down a murky whirlpool, washed away in a tide of delirium.

Oceans rose and sank. Skies ripped open and were pierced by flaming thunderbolts. Volcanoes spewed molten death and poisonous fumes. Blazing fires raced across the world, billowing sky-eating plumes of roiling black clouds. Drought parched entire landscapes. Deluges flooded the land and stripped it bare. Shifting ground shook and roared. Gigantic waves washed endlessly back and forth over my soul. Everything died, then rotted, then struggled to be reborn, and died again. Darkness, despair, and infinite time wasted my soul and I slept the sleep of the dead.

"Not bad," was all Mary Duneflower commented. "Have some coffee. Now I will tell you the history of the Sand Coast clans."

Chapter 3 — Beyond Old

Bloodied, beaten and cowed, the surviving remnants of the warriors of the Water Edge People staggered back into the bonfire-lit village commons. They collapsed, spent, in the arms of their women, children and parents. Defiantly, but ultimately without consequence, Seal Spear, their leader, was the last to back his way upright into the circle of firelight. He dripped from head to toe with sweat and blood. His countenance showed neither fear nor hope, only resignation and stark awareness.

The forest around them thrashed with the movements of the warriors of the invading hordes and reverberated dreadfully with their indecipherable murmurs, clicks and grunts. Everyone expected, within moments, to die a horrible death.

"My people," Seal Spear's voice trembled with his last remaining courage. "Be brave. Remember now. Offer respect. Be one. We die together." Heeding their leader, each individual spoke farewell with their eyes, relived their lives, and remembered their heritage of nows.

Imminent death did not come then and there. The invading hordes chose not to annihilate them, not just yet. There was a harsh bark in the forest, and then the voices and noises around them faded. Their agony and fear was to be prolonged.

Beyond Old eventually stood up from where he had been sitting quietly on a woven reed mat under his hut's extended roof. He approached Seal Spear, his eyes shrouded with a faraway gaze into long and broad perspectives. The tribe had started to recover from the immediate shock of not being summarily slain. Those who were able tended to the wounds of the surviving men. Others grieved without restraint. Seal Spear had not moved; he only peered into the dark wall of bushes that surrounded the village as the sounds of the others faded and the reality of their situation settled onto his shoulders.

"Brave man, wise leader, you no longer hunt seals with your spears." Like all the tribe's members, Seal Spear had edgy respect for their shaman, Beyond Old. Such attitudes did not include affection. Their shaman was much, much, too old and unearthly for that. The shamans of other tribes were healers and visionaries, powerful but mortal. The Water Edge People tolerated a seeming immortal as their intermediary with the sacred realms.

"Tell me then, old one, what kind of creatures are these, full of greed-fat, that I should be hunting with my spear?"

Beyond Old frowned. These new invaders were not just a new or different people; they had thoughts that were alien and dangerous. They believed that if they controlled the resources of a place, then they actually owned that part of the world as if they had made it themselves. How peculiar, when it was so obvious that all beings are born out of the world and are simply a part of its flowing web of birth, death, and rebirth. Did these others consider themselves to be gods, that they were separate from the cycle of creation and the fullness of coexistence?

"I have lived many years, but have no wisdom to confront this mind disease, leader Spear. Their thoughts are like the sicknesses that spread from touch to touch, bite to bite, breath to breath. Their ideas breed illness, violent death, and the loss of ancient respectful ways. It is sad and horrific to lose our loved ones here and now, but these ill-will tribes threaten our people with a final end. My counsel has changed. We must leave."

The shaman's radical shift in opinion jolted Seal Spear from his shock at the night's trauma. Although completely unexpected, Seal Spear reflected, the shaman's new pronouncement came none too soon.

Beyond Old had been so fixed to this place that he might as well be the oldest tree with the deepest roots. He not only was their healer, dream-visionary and life-guide; he was the incarnation of their view of reality. Their code of living was so simply put and so often repeated that it had become their view of the world. It was their tribal creed. He had taught it to each generation from childhood.

We are one, part of the whole
Our lives are a collection of now moments
Therefore we live with respect and compassion
To honor all existence
Here, on the water's edge

But how could such a code of thought, living, and place face the madmen of greed and still survive?

"So late you shift your stance, O rooted one. Too late? Can we still escape?"

"Your perspective and mine differ, Blubber Spear," Beyond Old ridiculed heedlessly, "but more considerations are at stake than your limited view can encompass."

Seal Spear was offended by both the direct insult and the disparagement, but he was too drained to respond in kind. Maybe so, but his people bleed in this now. Ten of his friends were dead. The other warriors were sorely wounded. Cherished women were made widows, and children fatherless. Even if they did migrate elsewhere, there would be few hunters to fill their bellies for many years to come. Hunger might heighten one's appreciation for the nature of reality while meditating, but only until starvation set in. Where exactly would they go? The bitter North?

"We will speak of your shifting wisdom soon, long-rotting man. First we lick our wounds and mourn our dead. Then you will tell all of us what you now believe. You have had many ages to think your thoughts. Speak well at our next council or be useless."

Seal Spear turned, finally embracing his wife Twisted Pine and son One Gull. They had approached him timidly in the aftermath of the tragedy, fearful of interrupting his council with the ancient shaman, but needing his solace. The family walked away together, holding each other in silence.

Beyond Old mused more.

∫

All the members of the tribe understood that drastic change was descending on their days and they could not wait long to decide their course of action. Two nights later, everyone gathered in the lodge of the people's body. Every age, both genders, any status, healthy or infirm, they shuffled in with worried faces and whispered comments. They numbered 70 in all, with only eight strong men who were all wounded but likely to recover.

Seal Spear sat in the leader's spot, his countenance grave. Beyond Old perched to his left and below, but still prominently in front. Many individuals had smeared their bodies with seal fat and ashes in their mourning. Hair was cut or torn out, clothes rent. The lodge fires were dim and smoky, smoldering under heaps of the sacred tribute herbs.

When the moment came, Seal Spear opened the meeting with the tribal creed, spoken with conviction, as always. All joined him intoning it, but mostly their words were spoken in half-hearted murmurs. Who could blame them?

"Speak!" he asserted, and the discussion was opened to all. It was critically important that each individual had a say if they wished, as much of a say as they desired, and for as long as they wanted. When the opinionated and wordy ones ran out of energy, then the weaker and more timid ones also would have their say. The discussion would continue as long as it took. Seal Spear would not allow any to leave until all who wished to express their thoughts had done so fully. Everyone knew and accepted this, so they generally kept their comments short and to the point.

This time there was not much debate, only agony and uncertainty.

"Our wondrous pines on the edge of the big sunrise water are a land of death now. Will we dwell here still?"

"We have always eaten well here, we have always lived in beauty here, but we cannot stop the others from killing us. Do we simply lie down and die?"

"If my man had drowned in the sea, or if he had died in bed as an old man, then his spirit would dwell with us in peace. Now he has been yanked away by evil invaders and this is no longer my home."

"This recent collection of nows does not feed our practice of compassion. Let us find new nows elsewhere that do."

Eventually silence descended on the group. Seal Spear waited. No one had addressed the central issue. Where were they to go? Their boats had never found new land eastwards into the waters. The greedy ones were invading from the south and west. They could move north along the water's edge, but in that direction laid bitter cold and the larger, more dangerous animals that they did not know how to hunt.

After a proper wait, Seal Spear broached the topic. "We must migrate north." His pronouncement, intended to stimulate debate, was met with absolute silence. No one looked at another.

After further consensual silence, Beyond Old finally spoke. "I have been to the northlands. It was many lives ago." Everyone quietly gasped. Many lives ago? Beyond Old was confirming their worst fears and rumors. He had lived longer than anyone in the tribe. Indeed several living elders remembered long dead grandparents who had known him personally when he was a middle-aged man. He still appeared only moderately old. Now he had mentioned previous lives! It lent credence to their worst whispered secret legends, passed through many generations; that he had started this life when his previous body had died and his mind had possessed a young boy-child.

Beyond Old was not oblivious to their fear. His words had been intentional and precise. He needed to shock the tribe into fear and focused action if he was to assume the risk that migration held for him. They must be strongly motivated to succeed. Or else he might not.

"Before I was the shaman for our people, I was a young man, carefree, curious, and prone to wandering. I explored south, but the land was full of nasty creatures and tribes that knew only self-indulgence and sloth. I explored to the west, but the land was dry and trampled by seasonal waves of grazing animals and tribes that always moved. Then I explored northwards. Our beloved pines, cedars, and oaks are soon replaced by somber firs and spruces and then by the snow white birches that grow ever shorter as one proceeds. Farther on, the winter winds, deep snows, and short summers eventually allow only the grasses, short berry shrubs, and colorful rock eaters to flourish. In the water, as on the land, the animals grow larger and roam vast distances to find their sustenance. Our gentle deer double in size and have antlers like trees. Then, farther still, they become shaggy with thick fur to survive the winter. Our shy bears become as large as four such here, are white, and fear no man or beast. Where seals inhabit our coasts, the water's edge to the north is populated with the sea lions and walruses we seldom see. There is plenty of game to hunt, but the animals become increasingly difficult and dangerous to stalk. I saw grazing beasts so large they could eat this lodge. They had bigger tails in front than in back, huge upward-curved ivory tusks bigger than those of a walrus, and they walked like mountains on the earth."

"In mid-summer, the day never ends. The sun barely dips below the rim of the earth as it skims around its edge. In mid-winter, the sun only peaks above the rim of the world briefly in the south for a few hours each day. The winter cold and the wind are unimaginable. Often, on a clear winter's night, the northern sky swims with several subtle colors of the rainbow, painted in delicate undulating waves across the heavens. I have never seen such beauty before or since."

"I traveled far along the edge of the water for three years and met no one, although I did find the rings of very old campfires. Other people had been there before but had not stayed, or perhaps, had not survived. As I continued, the land along the edge of the water gradually bent eastwards until I was traveling directly toward the new sun along our same great water that now lay to the south. That is when I chose to return to my people, to my tribe, to you."

They were all stunned, even Seal Spear. Beyond Old had never spoken of this before. No one else had explored more than a half-moon's travel north. Why should anyone do so until now? What had driven this crazy shaman to undertake such a solitary journey in his youth, whenever that was? Why had he never described the northern sojourn until now? Why was he inventing fanciful creatures?

Beyond Old had personal reasons for his reticence.

Migrating along the northern edge of the great water toward the uncertain possibility of new tribal lands in a far distant south that might not exist posed immense risks to his longevity. Yet he judged almost certain death at the hands of crazed greed-warriors to be worse. The time had come to lead the tribe elsewhere. This was the only possibility. He loved his tribe with a depth of experience beyond compare. His collection of nows was immense, but if the tribe did not survive, what would it matter if he continued to live? Whatever his tribe might think of him, longevity did not derive from invulnerability.

"Seal Spear can lead you as we begin our tribe's far wander. I can help along the way. I have learned how to live along the cold northern edge of the water. Maybe, just maybe, the land along the water will once again bend to the south beyond where I last traveled. Perhaps our tribe can once again find warmer climes, seal and deer among new pines, cedars and oaks on another edge of the water. If not, we can learn to live in the north."

"The tribe must move slowly at first as we learn to hunt and live in the cold lands. We need a new generation of strong young hunters to succeed in our long exodus through the challenging northlands. Maybe your grandchildren will see such new southlands if they exist. If not, your offspring could become the new tribe of the north."

"Here is my vision. I have wandered far in my dreams. I have seen a new dwelling place on an edge of the great water that faces the sunset. None of you will live to see this place. It is too far. Nor will this old man. We will become the Trodders of the Far Mist, a new tribe. Our distant descendants will live in new lands, but at least we will have descendants. That is my counsel."

No one liked his counsel, but the people chose to go. No choice is a choice.

$$\int$$

"Come with me. Take my hand." Beyond Old enticed One Gull. "Let us walk on the edge of the water and talk together as one."

At five years of age, One Gull was not in a position to refuse the tribe's shaman his request. They departed in the early morning mist before his parents noticed he was missing. Beyond Old led him by long winding and sheltered paths that One Gull had never passed before to an isolated stretch of shoreline that was hidden by high cliffs and dense trees. Here was a cove that echoed with powerful waves and the barking of seals. The early summer day was warm and humid, yet blustery. One Gull's namesake birds etched patterns across the sky. In spite of his limited awareness, he felt big changes approaching him, like a wave that reached to the sky.

They strolled along the strand. Beyond Old began, "Your mother, Twisted Pine, and your father, Seal Spear, are my blood family, One Gull. Yet, they do not know it. You are my offspring too. You are my descendant through many families." Beyond Old knew that One Gull could understand little of what he spoke, but that such information was nonetheless helpful for an effective jump.

Continuing, Beyond Old instructed, "Our tribe must soon leave for new lands. I am too old to journey so far in this body. To be of use to our tribe, I must have a new body."

"Like a deer or a seal?" the youth asked.

"No, I must be another person of our tribe."

"I do not understand, Old One."

"Come, let me show you a sacred place. This place is where I was BORN."

At the far end of the cove, Beyond Old led One Gull up a sinuous steep track to a bluff overlooking the water. In a sandy nook on the headlands there was a flat place sheltered by a small grove of stunted oaks.

"Wait here. This is a very special place. Think of now."

One Gull sat looking out over the endless water. His belly wanted food. He wanted his mother and father. The old man frightened him.

Soon, Beyond Old returned and sat next to him. "Here, are you hungry?" The shaman had brought some yellow-stemmed, spotted, ground-fleshes that he had just collected. The tribe often ate these sorts of growths, but usually they cooked them. Eating them raw was not appealing. The old man insisted, and ate some too.

While they sat together, the Old Man started to intone some ritual phrases, his arms raised to the water.

One Gull, puzzled, caught snatches of meaning from words that seemed old and odd, as if the roots of common words were spat, one next to another, without the flow of common talk. He heard meanings such as, "now again together," "long vision to me," "blood to blood," "new body, new mind" and "grant this jump."

One Gull swooned. The world shifted. He was no longer alone in his thoughts, in his skull.

One Gull swooned. The world shifted. He was no longer alone
in his thoughts, in his skull.

A mountain of ideas settled on him, became him.

What happened next was not for One Gull to describe. Eventually, late in the day, he returned to the village, but Beyond Old did not.

The next day, One Gull led the tribe to the dead shaman's body. "What One Gull?" his parents beseeched him. "Where is he leading us?" others asked. "What is this place that One Gull has found?" They found Beyond Old reclined as if he had fallen asleep peacefully, overlooking the edge of the water. "Finally deceased!? Really?"

The ceremony that ushered the shaman to the next world was awkward and unfulfilling to all who participated. Why had the ancient Beyond Old mysteriously fled in the hour of their need? How would they find a new warm edge of the great water now?

Strangely, One Gull had seen him last; why was the young boy so quiet? Why were his eyes so deep, his demeanor so mature?

∫

Shortly before the tribe embarked on their perilous journey, One Gull snuck off along the hidden forest paths again, visiting the sacred oak grove of his transcendence. Nearby, he collected the knobby, shelf-like, stretching rot-fleshes that grew on the boles of ancient pure-heart cedars.

He gathered as many as he could find and hid them in his travel pack. Maybe, just maybe, they would suffice to see him to a new world by prolonging this body's life. Maybe he could lead his people there before this body died.

Unfortunately, only freshly picked jumping ground-fleshes were effective and he doubted that the oaks where they grew would be found along their sojourn. The longer one lived, the harder death was to accept.

The tribe set forth and traveled far. Their journey took six generations. Often they would settle for years at a time to hunt, renew their supplies, fix their boats, craft new weapons, breed new hunters, care for their elderly, and bury the deceased. Many were the hardships and trials they endured. Huge bears, fierce wolves, giant game, sea monsters. They even hunted the two-tailed lodges-on-legs. No one doubted their shaman's tales now.

Old One Gull urged them on, again and yet again, usually before they wished to leave. The land eventually did bend south. The tribe eventually did enter warmer lands. More often the people wanted to stop and settle. This place or the next was good enough. Indeed the new lands were lush with all they needed to live abundantly and the climate was not too harsh. Still, no place they found was yet good enough for the aging shaman Old Gull. He pressed them ever onwards with his assurances of a promised land like unto that of their distant ancestors. Ancestors they no longer remembered, except in winter stories the shaman told. Finally, the "Trodders of the Far Mist," the "Far Wanderers" as they called themselves now, came to the land of the shaman's primordial dreams. Pines, oaks, and pure-heart cedars grew on the edge of the water that faced west.

As they had suspected from evidence along the way, other people already dwelled here. The others were not numerous, but to Beyond Old Gull's dismay, they lived in the hills where the oaks grew. The shaman felt increasingly desperate. He was very aged and becoming feeble again. His supply of stretching rot-fleshes was exhausted and he had only now found new pure-heart cedars upon which they might grow. But they only delayed aging anyway. Without access to more of the jumping ground-fleshes that he had only found under certain oaks, how was he to live again?

Chapter 4 — Poor Fens

"WATCH OUT!" Wally made like a toppling tree as Grace dove to the ground underneath his outstretched boot and hunkered protectively over something. Checking his tumble involved slamming a recently shined cowboy boot down into a pile of fresh, steaming, huckleberry-infused, bear dung and flailing with his arms into a brittle-limbed manzanita bush that ripped the sleeve of his new, brightly patterned, pearl-snap, rodeo-styled cowboy shirt. He was not a happy camper, or rather, field trip participant.

Grace looked up, oblivious to Wally's annoyance, and declared imperiously, "This is a globally-endangered western lily you almost stepped on! It is on Federal and State endangered species lists and the BLM's sensitive species roster. There are only a few populations in the entire world and you just about squashed one of them!"

Stan could not hide his distain for this ridiculous display of lily-livered eco-extremism. It should have been a bleeding heart that Wally almost smashed! Twarn noted that Grace's voice could be quite shrill when she was upset. Bugs shook his head and collected some moss that Wally could use to clean his boot. The morning rains had ended

and the hot late afternoon sun was causing steam to rise off
the wet bushes. As Ole approached the group, he could
have sworn that some of the vapor rising behind Wally's
head was actually coming out of his ears. He was certainly a
red man.

"Crap! You'd think I about stepped on a pristine
plover's egg! It's not even blooming, so how would I know
anyway? Get up off your knees and show some dignity,"
Wally shot back as he cringed at his own lack of
composure. Although his words were harsh, Grace had
always been one of Wally's favorite young tribal members.
Her mother had died delivering her and she lost her father
several years later when his fishing boat capsized in a winter
storm. Grace had subsequently been adopted and raised by
Wally's aunt and tribal elder, Mary Duneflower. That made
Grace his younger cousin by adoption, although he was old
enough to be her dad. Wally was especially proud of her
sobriety and motivation. During senior year in high school,
she had obtained her own scholarship to attend the
prestigious private Lewis and Clark College in Portland.
While attending, she had worked on archaeological sites
throughout the Northwest to supplement her scholarship
funds and had graduated with honors and a B.S. in
Anthropology. Subsequently, she rapidly earned a M.S.,
specializing in paleoecology, whatever that was. Now she
had a great job with the Oregon Office of The
Conservancy. He had reason to be proud of her, but he also
had reason to be very aggravated.

"I heard dat Indian moms used ta stuff dis inta dose
baby carriers. Mother Nature's pampers." Bugs joked as he
pointed to Wally's boot and handed him the moss.

"Umpin-atem, missy," he cheerfully chimed as he lent Grace a hand up and gave her a good-natured wink. Bugs might have his own reasons to be aggravated with Grace, but that was no reason to forgo courtesy.

Grace was brushing the sand off her pants and Wally was wiping his boot, when Stan suddenly stomped off through a gap in the bushes voicing loud invectives against "enviro-terrorists" and "nature-fascists."

"What the..." Grace started, but the blank curious stares she saw on everyone's faces suggested it was a useless question. Shortly they all caught up with Stan, but no one got too close because he looked like he was about to commit an act of violence with the wooden stake he was slapping against one of his palms.

"Its ilk like you who incite those earth-libbers to destroy private property!" Stan shouted at Grace. "I'd like to cement them into the foundations of my resort buildings and you ... you ... NATURE CONSERVERS should be locked up for egging them on!" Stan was definitely not an Indian, but it was now his turn to be a red man.

Ole, unafraid of Stan, and quite disgusted with his childish display, simply walked over and took the stake from the man before he thought to react.

"You can see over there where it was originally stuck in the ground, Stan. Likely as not, it was a curious deer that dislodged it by tasting the red paint on top. I don't see any other boot prints out here and I doubt anyone is messing with your surveyor's stakes. In any case, your employee needs more practice. I believe this stake is on my property, not the tribe's."

"Yeah, chill," said Grace to Stan. She was none too

happy about the verbal lashings she had just been getting.

Stan whirled on her and shouted at the top of his lungs, "Chill yourself, you brown-butted nature freak!"

Now Wally re-reddened. Although he had commissioned Stan's land development company, Hidden Lakes Real Estate, to plan a casino for the tribe, racial slurs were extremely inappropriate, especially aimed at his favorite cousin!

Fortunately, Ole was now holding the stake because Wally was twice Stan's size and started to approach him threateningly.

Grace quickly composed herself and intervened, "Wally, NO! Let it go."

Turning to Stan: "I'm sorry, telling you to chill was not nice of me."

To the group: "I think we all need a break; how about lunch?"

The new mantra for solutions to environmental conflicts was to involve all stakeholders and to try to reach a consensus solution that all interests would support. Huh, thought Grace, as she sought a comfortable place in the sun to sit for lunch, let's see those starry-eyed conflict resolution idealists deal with this group of men!

Oh, to be sure, Bugs always seemed amused, Ole humble, and Twarn quiet, but finding a lick of common ground among these characters was going to be a challenge. If she could pull it off and find a way to preserve this incredibly unique habitat, it would be a huge feather in her career hat with The Conservancy. She had been in town for nearly a year now, working to find a win-win solution to a controversy that had been festering and building to a head since last autumn's cranberry festival. She hoped to find a way to conserve the fragile bog lands while also accommodating the community's economic development needs in the form of the JCBEP and Indian Casino. She actually had to furtively threaten Stan, Wally, and Bugs to get them to come on this field trip to explain the Conservancy's point of view.

"Gentlemen, when we file our appeal of your various development plans with the Conservation Division of the State Department of Natural Resources, wouldn't you like to know in advance what our arguments will be?"

The coercion was veiled in the form of a question, but just barely.

"No, I am not going to share a draft copy that might be misquoted or prematurely distributed. If you want to know what we are concerned about, you will just have to come out there with me and see for yourself!"

Fortunately, her threatening suggestion had succeeded. She could think of no better way to educate these fools about what they were planning to rip up and flood, or to plow under and pave.

Twarn had settled next to Grace and she turned to him. "Thanks so much for coming, Twarn. I'm sorry to drag you into this controversy, but I think these guys will listen more closely to another man than they will to me. After all, you have a stake in this too." Twarn Thongchai just smiled modestly and nodded to himself as he delved into his lunch sack.

Stan, still fuming, snipped sarcastically, "Yeah, big stake, too lazy to grow your own mushrooms, eh? Rather pick them from someone else's property?"

If there was one type of person for whom Ole lacked tolerance, it was those who refused to grow up.

"Twarn has always obtained permission to pick mushrooms on my land."

"From the tribe too," Wally inserted.

"Not only that," Ole continued, "but Twarn has proved his value many times over by alerting me to trespassers who hunt, fish, pick mushrooms, tear around in dune buggies, start dangerous campfires, deface signs, vandalize equipment, dump trash, or stick stakes on my property. Best of all, he shares many of the mushrooms he can't sell with me and my friends. I wish everyone was so responsible and generous."

"Dat's right" Bugs added, "Twarn is also a mighty schmart man! Bonny and me thought ve knew all der vus ta know 'bout mushrooms, but Twarn learned us a ding or two! I ain't never seen a man vhat knew more 'bout dis here svampland and all da critters."

"Which is precisely why I invited him." said Grace.

"So just how did you learn so much, Twarn?" Stan groused. Silence ensued as Twarn composed his thoughts and the group ate, waiting for him to respond.

"I was born on the Mae Nom Kong, or Mekong River, on the border between Thailand and Laos. Other than a general sense of chaos and conflict, I don't remember much of my youth. The moments I remember best were by contrast, peaceful. I fondly recall meandering through the forest with my mother and her friends to collect mushrooms and other herbs. War eventually came to the village, as did both local fighters and Americans. Some of the Americans stayed for a while and one eventually fell in love with my mother. My father had disappeared in the war, so she married the American and we moved to San Francisco when I was five."

"I was a Navy pilot in Vietnam. Good thing you weren't a gook, or you wouldn't be here now." Everyone stared aghast at Stan. Did this guy have even a strand of decency?

Twarn ignored him and simply continued, "My new American father had become a junkie during the war and he OD'ed five years later. Before long, I was working to support my mother, but she kept encouraging me to stay in school and better myself. I tried … hard. I was always drawn to the natural world, so I eventually graduated from the University of California at Berkeley with a Ph.D. in Plant Ecology. I started to teach at San Francisco State University, but mom died a few years later. In my grief, I realized I had really just done it all for her. I couldn't personally care less about advanced degrees and high-paying jobs behind a desk or in front of a lectern. I had led several plant ecology field trips to the southern Oregon coast during my teaching stint, and had fallen in love with the area. I had a small inheritance from the family of my American father. I had also saved a little money of my own. I chose to move here and live simply. Picking mushrooms provides me with the income I need and the peaceful forests remind me therapeutically of my mother and my homeland.

"So now you tromp through the rain for hours on end and hang out at blue-tarped mushroom buying sheds for half the year, while you veg out on welfare the other half. Sounds like a great life."

Wally had had his fill and towered over Stan before anyone could react. "If you don't APOLOGIZE NOW, I will personally see to it that you lose the tribe's casino contract and that you have nothing to do with the most lucrative development on the South Coast!"

Stan momentarily cowered. Twarn waved Wally to back off. "He's right mostly, except the welfare part."

"Let's get on with this, shall we?" Stan deflected their ire. "I've got sand in my pants, the sun is sinking lower, and I sure as dickens don't want to walk out of this miasmal swamp in the dark."

"Good idea, Stan," Grace encouraged, "Twarn, would you be so kind as to enlighten these individuals about the unique qualities of this place?" Stan's sarcasm was getting contagious.

"I'll try to keep it fairly short, but after all, this information is for your benefit." Even Twarn, it seemed, was not beneath subtle sarcasm, and everybody GOT IT.

"This area is special for three interrelated reasons. One, the combination of climate, geology, and hydrology is unique. Two, the ecosystems that have evolved here are very old and very stable. And three, this age-old sheltered habitat has allowed a variety of rare species to persist only here."

"Let's start with the coastal climate. Inland fossil pollen records for the last 10,000 years, that is, since the last glaciation, show alternating periods of hot dry weather and cold wet weather, each lasting centuries at a time. However, right along the coast, proximity to the ocean lessens these extremes and vegetation does not need to respond by shifting north or south to remain adapted to the climate."

"What about ocean levels, haven't they risen a lot since the glaciers melted?" Bugs interjected.

Smiling—he still loved tit for tat with students—Twarn responded, "Yes they have, but this portion of the Oregon coast near Bandon has experienced tectonic uplift paralleling the rise in ocean levels such that this area has never been inundated since humans started inhabiting it."

"The geology is related to the hydrology. This area that is so conducive to both natural and cranberry bogs, drains poorly because it is perched on the Whiskey Run Terrace. The terrace is a thick layer of consolidated sediment, up to 500 feet deep in places, that was deposited over 10,000 years ago during the last glaciation of the Pleistocene Ice Age. The salient feature though, is the fact that it has a layer of partially cemented clay 1-10 feet below the surface. This natural hardpan inhibits water infiltration, thus causing water to collect at or near the soil surface, rather than draining into aquifers."

"Hardpan," noted Stan, stomping on the ground, "sounds like a solid foundation for buildings!"

"Sure, if you like houseboats!" Grace stomped back, pointing out the water oozing into each footprint.

Stan really didn't need the reminder. Unlike Grace, Twarn, Ole, and Bugs, he and Wally had not worn waterproof foot ware.

"Please!" Twarn interjected. "Follow me." He continued. "John Kirkpatrick was an early European explorer of this area. He was one of the survivors of the conflict at Battle Rock in 1851. He led a group of men through this area and described it as a great swamp that was dominated by large expanses of water containing wet meadows, backwater marshland, spruce swamps and a network of small creeks, lakes and rivers. It was an accurate description of poor drainage. I brought along an excerpt from his journal. And I quote:

"...about three o'clock the next day, we came to the edge of what seemed to us a large plain. It looked to be miles in extent, and was covered with a heavy growth of high grass, and proved to be an immense swamp. We now determined to try and cross this swamp and reach the sea after dark and travel all night. We floundered around in this swamp all night, sometimes in water up to our armpits, until after dark we found a little island about an acre of dry land and covered with a thick growth of small fir bushes. Here we laid down and tried to rest and sleep but encountered a new enemy in the shape of clouds of mosquitoes."

"Right!" responded Stan, growing impatient. "Another reason to get out of here before dusk!"

"If you let him get on with it, maybe we will," Bugs suggested mildly, but this time the twinkle in his eye had an edge to it.

"Over here, take a look, this is a classic Whiskey Terrace bog. Most of the bogs here are actually old lakes. Technically speaking, as a lake fills in with decaying organic matter, bog plants colonize the edge."

"So what exactly is a bog, technically speaking that is?" asked Ole. He had been so quiet, that everyone looked at him. He shrugged. "That definition doesn't fit our cranberry bogs."

Again, Twarn smiled and launched into his explanation. "Great question, Ole. Classically bogs are defined as wet areas with no drainage, filled with rainwater only, very acidic, very low in nutrients, and accumulating peat from moss that doesn't decay completely."

"Then what are swamps or swales?" Even Bugs was getting into the teacher/student mode now. These definitions, after all, were pertinent to his livelihood. He was hesitant to discuss CFA's plans for the JCBEP with this group, but he did want to understand the environmental terminology better so they had a better chance of addressing appeals.

"Ah, well, most of the terms for wetlands," continued Twarn professorially, "derive from northern Europe where such areas are common and academics have had a long time to argue about definitions. Let's see; swales are slight depressions, on otherwise level ground, that become seasonally inundated. Marshes are periodically inundated, but not necessarily seasonally; for instance, tidal marshes. They usually overlie mineral-rich substrates with nutrient-rich water, and do not accumulate peat. Swamps are often forested and also occur on mineral soils with nutrient-rich water. A moor is a boggy wasteland with heather, bracken, sedge or peat moss. Think Hound of the Baskervilles. A fen is a bog with some stream input, some drainage, some nutrients, and not quite as acidic as a bog. It does have mosses that form peat, but usually different species than those found in a true bog. A carr is a fen that has more shrubby or woody plants. A mire is any peat-forming wetland. A palustrine ecosystem, such as the one found here, is a wet land-locked, non-tidal area without much drainage or open water."

"OK, Ok, ok. Enough already! I'm getting mired down by all these pickyun definitions!" Plucking his soaked shoe out of a particularly sticky spot, Stan asked a question of his own. "So then what is all this sucking muck?"

"Muck," continued Twarn without missing a beat, "is dark, finely divided, well decomposed, organic matter deposited on the surface in poorly drained areas."

Bugs had this funny habit of doubling over with laughter, but he did the best he could to control it.

"Actually," Twarn pressed his point, "we don't even have true bogs here. They should really be classified as poor fens. They have a little bit of drainage, but they are still very nutrient-poor and acidic."

Stan sneered. "Then it doesn't matter if the tribe or the CFA drains the bogs anyway, because they are only poor fenny-wennies!"

Grace struggled to suppress her mental image of where to thrust a toe of her new stiff hiking boots.

"All very interesting. What does it matter?" Wally was not being sarcastic. He had been listening closely, but he still didn't get how this all affected the tribe's casino plans. Bogs were bogs, even if they were poor fens. Either could be drained.

"Uniquely ancient, and ancient uniqueness." It seemed Twarn had a short concise answer for everything. He should have been a one-liner marketing exec.

"You see," he continued, "all natural ecosystems get set back by disturbance and go through a process called succession where one community of organisms replaces another until a state of equilibrium is reached called a climax community. Usually, even if such mature and self-maintaining communities evolve, they don't last long because another disturbance comes along. Examples include wildfires, drought, wind, floods, volcanoes, etc. Then the ecosystem gets reset and succession starts over again with the species that are adapted to disturbed conditions. Some climax communities can last for several thousands of years, such as old-growth redwood, sequoia, or Bishop pine forests. Many only last for a few decades or centuries. Some of these coastal bog ecosystems may have experienced little change in the 12,000 years it takes a lake to become a bog!"

"No way," quipped Stan.

"Way," counter-quipped Grace. They exchanged lingering glares.

"In a stable climate, like here on the coast, peat accumulates at a rate of about 1 inch every 40 years. Peat deposits at Wohanik Lake, just north of here, are thought to be the result of 12,000 years of deposition. The vegetation in and around these bogs has probably been relatively stable for as long as humans have been here. That's enough time for these unique plants, fungi, and other organisms to become highly specialized and adapted to this ecosystem."

Twarn saw that Stan was opening his mouth again, so he hurried on. "And, that is precisely what you all need to be concerned about!"

The field trip members had been meandering along a saturated stream bank as Twarn expounded, but now they all pulled up short and turned to listen more closely. He was coming to the crux of the litigation and regulation issues that would affect them all.

"The unique hydrology, lack of nutrients, and stable environment here constitutes an environment found in few other places on the planet. In addition to the super-rare lily you almost stepped on Wally, there are sixteen other rare species growing on the landscape you hope to drain and develop. Not only are there endangered plants, there are rare and endangered plant communities. The 'bog blueberry-tufted grass-shrub/swamp' is considered globally imperiled."

"Bog Blueberries!" Stan couldn't help himself. "Blueberries aren't imperiled!"

Sighing to himself, Twarn explained. "Common names are fraught with peril. I was referring to a native bog species that is related to, but different from, either blueberries or cranberries. In this case, the species is part of a plant community that occurs almost no place else on earth. Believe me, lots of people care about this!"

"Oh, I believe you," Stan fumed, "I just can't comprehend why anyone would care about collections of stinking bog plants when there is money to be made! What idiots…Oh, MUCK!" Stan got distracted by not watching where he stepped.

"It gets worse Stan, or better, as I believe. Let's talk trees, lichens, and fungi now. Let me show you the most unusual bog I know. Ole, do you mind if we visit the ancient grove?"

It was a simple setup. Ole and Twarn had discussed it. Ole was not too keen on the word getting around, especially after the night in question. Still, he had been moved by Twarn's information, and he wanted these folks to understand his recent change of heart about draining more bogs.

"Nope," Ole responded.

Bugs eyed him, but Ole just inclined his head toward the natural bog they had been walking towards several months ago along the nutria-infested berm. The Bog Maiden Bog! Shades of Stankiewicz! He finally figured it out.

As they approached, Twarn continued to spew. Would the guy never cease his tirade of meaningless nature-facts, thought Stan. He sounds worse than a PBS special about the intrinsic worth of snail darters. This time though, he kept his mouth shut.

"If there was ever a perfect movie spot for a spooky bog sequence, this would be it. See that dark stuff draping off all the tree limbs surrounding the bog? That is the rare horsehair lichen *Bryoria spiralifera*."

"Whatsia?" Stan belittled Twarn's use of botanical Latin, unable to restrain himself.

"Oh, sorry, I have been trying my best to avoid confusing you all with precise scientific terms. The point is that this lichen has a very narrow range of conditions where it can grow, and it is endangered by development throughout its range, and it grows most luxuriantly in this one particular grove of old trees next to this one particular bog. It might seem ghastly and spooky, but there is nothing like it remaining anywhere else on earth!"

Yet again Twarn cut off Stan as he started to speak. "I'm not done! This bog, like others nearby, is surrounded by plants adapted to very low nutrient conditions. The hooded insectivorous pitcher plant *Darlingtonia californica* eats bugs because the soil and water can't sustain it. Port Orford cedars grow around the edge of the bog because they are adapted to nutrient poor soils. Both are relatively widespread in southern Oregon and northern California."

"So?" Stan.

"So this!" Twarn. He was pointing at a shelf fungus with odd stubs protruding underneath, growing out from the notch of a dead limb on a very old Port Orford cedar.

"So?" Stan.

"So…" Twarn led in slowly, "this is a species of fungus, that, to my knowledge, has never been described. I discovered it. Do you think I should tell the world about it?"

Stan was not so flippant now. He said nothing.

"It is in the genus *Echinodontium*. Most species in the genus are uncommon. On the East Coast, there is only one species and it only infects old Atlantic white cedar trees that grow in bogs. The fungus was thought to be extinct as a result of lumbering old trees. Recently, an intrepid pair of mycological sleuths tromped out onto a frozen remnant bog one winter and rediscovered a few conks on a few old trees."

"Atlantic white cedars are in the genus *Chamaecyparis*, the same as Port Orford cedars. Another species of *Echinodontium* can be found on high elevation true firs and mountain hemlocks in the West, but none has ever been found on Port Orford cedars before. My guess is that this particular fungus requires very humid conditions, and very old trees to infect, and that is why it grows only here."

Ole was antsy. He had not discussed this fungus with Twarn. The others were fidgeting too. The day was getting late, and they still felt like they were in the middle of nowhere facing a long hike out. Ole had not bothered to inform them that a hundred yards away they would exit onto his highway-like bog-divider berms and stroll out easily, even in the descending dusk (barring voracious nose-nippers, of course).

"Now, the coup de grâce!" proclaimed Twarn.

"The who de grass?" flipped Stan, irritated and puzzled.

"Stanley, sir," chided Twarn as he shifted to his finale, "There are two more species here that I believe have never been described before and that might not grow anywhere else!"

Stan just fumed. Wally paid attention. Bugs couldn't help but be interested. Grace felt it was a slam-dunk.

"Over here. Tread carefully. Please don't step on the mushrooms." Twarn did his best to impart a sense of entering a sacred space. "You see, I know of no other trees like these."

Even befuddled obtusers like Stan thought that this was a creepy place. It felt like it was straight out of a Pixar Studios CG virtualization of a druid shrine. He tried to hide his uneasiness with a snide, "Oooo, deeply creepy!"

"What are these, oaks?" asked Wally. "Oaks don't grow on the dunes."

"Ah," responded Twarn, "but these do."

"The leaves look like Oregon white oaks," said Grace. Even she was puzzled. "but I have never seen them grow in a short dome shaped clustered grove like this, and certainly not on the dunes."

"You are absolutely right Grace and Wally," Twarn responded, "Oregon white oak does have a form, or subspecies, that grows with multiple, clustered short trunks like this, but it is native to the northern Sierra range of

California, not the Oregon coast. There is another diminutive variety that grows as a marginal species in the Redwood forests of Northern California, but it usually grows as a solitary trunk. Oaks often form hybrid swarms however, so it can be difficult to discern their phylogeny from their morphology."

"Their what from their what?" Stan was approaching his limits and the rest silently concurred that this jargon was unnecessary.

"I believe that this grove of ancient oaks is a hybrid between our Oregon white oak and the deer oak that grows in the nearby Siskiyou Mountains. The deer oak is the most unusual oak in western North America. It is very closely related to Asian oaks and it also is adapted to acidic, nutrient-poor soil. I think this grove of oaks is like no other in North America. That applies to these yellow and red amanitas too!"

Twarn had adopted a pose. His left arm was akimbo, his torso leaned right, and, with a flourish of his right arm, he pointed dramatically at the glistening two-hued mushrooms. They weren't quite growing in a fairy ring, more like in overlapping arcs. They were fresh but full-grown; obviously, they had come up in a recent flush.

"You have probably all seen the fly amanita before, the one with the red cap and white spots," continued Twarn. "I don't even want to go into the history behind that mushroom. I could put whole audiences to sleep!"

Well, YEAH, they all thought.

"This mushroom is distinctly different." Twarn lowered his voice to a spooky whisper so they had to pay attention to hear him. Quiet eeriness filled his voice.

"See the yellow stem and the yellow spots on the red cap? No other *Amanita* mushroom has those characters. Amanitas are a type of mushroom that grows symbiotically with tree roots, so this exceptional mushroom is growing exclusively with this previously unknown tree. That makes three species that appear to inhabit only the edge of this particular bog! They probably grow nowhere else in the world. A conk, a tree, and a mushroom." In the growing gloom, Twarn lowered his voice yet a notch further and leaned toward the tightly gathered group as if to share a secret. "Care to inform the world of these splendid discoveries?"

On cue, an owl hooted. Hector chose that moment to appear from behind a tree and startled them all to various degrees.

"Wh-Who are you!?" accused Stan, more startled than he cared to admit, even to himself. He felt like a trapped itch that could only be scratched with an escape. He frantically swatted at a mosquito departing his face. The *Yuma myotis* bat that had been swooping back and forth above the bog eating copious quantities of resident bugs chose that moment to swoop on a blood-engorged target near Stan's head. Stan jerked backwards as the bat flew straight at his face and then veered through his hair at the last split second to snatch the plasma prize.

"How do we get out of here!?" he yipped with a tinge of panic.

Not wanting Stan to get hysterical or to start flinging ethnic slurs at his valued farm hand, Ole quickly piped up, "This is Hector Hernandez, my farm assistant. We are near the edge of my cranberry bogs. Hector can guide you along my berms to the highway."

"This way, por favor," Hector gestured, and then started walking out of the grove without looking back.

"You didn't think to tell us this before!" Stan scoffed as he blustered off and followed Hector closely.

Bugs had known where they were, but thought Stan's point was well taken. Wally just nonchalantly followed Hector and Stan. Twarn disappeared.

Ole stood still while Grace got on her knees and tried to repair the damage Stan had done to the mushrooms as he had hurriedly departed. Grace glanced at Ole in the gathering gloom. Neither said anything about her tears over the thoughtless disregard Stan had shown this special place. Unspoken also were their thoughts about their mutual acquaintance with Johnny Wanders and what happened here that particular night last summer.

So much had changed since she had reconnected with Johnny.

∫

"Hey Johnny."

"Hi Grace." After their warm embrace, they held on, leaned back, and gazed into each other's eyes for a few moments without speaking. Then he kissed her gently and let go.

"How was the nature trip?"

"Hmmm, 'trip' is a good word for it. I felt like I kept tripping over myself with impatience. That Stan is… No, I need to walk it off some before I talk about it. Still up for Sandstone?"

"Got my hiking boots on too," he pointed at his feet, "but I am a little surprised you are still up for some hiking after dark."

"Oh, we didn't walk that far through the dunes and bogs. Stan doesn't walk very fast off-pavement, so it was really more of a stroll. Anyway, the point is only a couple of miles round trip."

Sandstone Point was their favorite sunset spot on the south coast. It was great for romantic moonlight excursions too. Little known by outsiders and seldom visited by most locals, it was one of the most dramatic viewpoints around and usually offered privacy. They drove to the remote, poorly marked trailhead in silence. Johnny let Grace digest the day's events as he drove down the county road. The moon was one day away from being full and had crested the coastal mountains to the east, casting long scraggly fir shadows across the illuminated cranberry bogs en route.

Johnny pulled into the gravel parking space at the trailhead and they loaded a few provisions. "I brought some smoked salmon, cheese, French bread, and a couple of apples." he said.

"I grabbed a bottle of mamaw's famous fizzy huckleberry juice, a space blanket to sit on, and a couple of warm blankets to wrap around us." she replied.

"Only need one blanket to wrap around us," Johnny hinted.

Grace reached around his waist and squeezed. "Then the other will make sitting on the space blanket warmer."

"Whatever," Johnny winked.

The trail was fairly flat and easy going, but hikers had to pay attention, especially at night. Around every bend there seemed to be another puddle in the poorly drained path. The unwary could easily stumble over protruding roots. The first part of the trail had been cut like a straight-sided vertical swath through dense rhododendron, salal, wax myrtle, salmonberry, and evergreen huckleberry bushes that grew taller than their heads. Frequently errant branches protruded at eye-level. The beams from their headlamps bounced, swept, and crisscrossed as they made their way carefully along the obstacle course. It could be considered a minor nuisance or a simple challenge. Either way, the trail conditions kept casual strollers at bay.

The second half of the trail broke out into a Sitka spruce forest with an open understory of windswept grasses and low herbs. Ethereal moonlight filtered through the canopy in slanted shafts that intersected with the bright beams of their headlamps. They paused briefly to sit on the bench built by civic-minded volunteers and killed their lights to take in the ambiance and listen to the last of the summer crickets. The seat overlooked a perched swale that was lined with white-barked alders and filled with the huge leaves of skunk cabbage. The moonlight was barely bright enough to give a hint of a greenish tint to the gray skunk cabbage leaves, but the alders glowed like there was an elf behind each one, ready to leap out. Anxious to get to the point, and settle in for a view, they continued and soon found themselves overlooking the vast Pacific from several hundred feet above the waves.

It was a little risky, especially at night, to traverse part way out along the crumbling headland to their favorite viewpoint, but the moon was now higher in the sky and the destination was worth the scramble. They clambered down into a notch in the rocks on the south side of the ridge. The perch afforded a dramatic view of the cliffs, beach, waves, and moon to the south. Ridge boulders sheltered them from seaward winds and the notch had a flat sandy bottom large enough for spreading out a picnic tarp. Or whatever.

Actually, they did settle in for a moonlight picnic. Grace hadn't eaten much for lunch. Stan had interrupted her meal and ruined her appetite. Now she felt ravenous and dug in.

"Wow!" Johnny noted. "That is some bodacious huckleberry juice. Must take like forever to make."

"Mamaw loves to pick all kinds of berries, but this is my favorite juice. It's the love that she works into it that tastes so good." Grace hesitated. "So, Johnny, when was your last drink?"

Johnny replied nonchalantly, "About 10 seconds ago."

Grace frowned in feigned frustration and gave him a little poke with her forefinger, "I meant booze, silly!"

Johnny just looked at her, no silliness in his eyes. "Been a while." He looked back at the moonlight reflecting on the waves and she dropped it.

After eating and cooling down from the hike, they did snuggle together under one blanket and sat on the other, atop the space blanket tarp. They had still not made love. During high school, Grace had diligently resisted Johnny's ardent advances and juvenile attempts to convince her to have sex with him. She did not know what kinds of drugs he was getting into or whether he had other partners. She was not about to risk her future on a few tumbles in the sand at beach parties or awkward humps in the back seat of a car on a dark forest lane.

However, ever since they had reconnected at the Puddle Inn, he seemed a paragon of patience. Occasionally she would catch glimpses of wily coyote in his eyes, or notice words or comments that could be interpreted several ways, but that was just part of the fun of courtship. As her local work on the bog project had extended over many months, they saw each other often and had again become increasingly affectionate. Still, they both harbored deep reservations. Trust and acceptance grew slowly as they shared stories of their lives since high school. They both knew they were laying a foundation, but could not foresee what they might build upon it.

This is a whole lot nicer than vision quests, Johnny thought as he pondered his future and maybe their future. How much should I tell Grace about what happened that night, he wondered.

I'll never forget this night, Grace reflected, as waves of affection welled up in her for this enigmatic man next to her. Should I tell him what others have told me about the night of his vision quest at that extraordinary bog? Should I encourage him on his path? Do I want to share it with him?

All their thoughts floated between them, unspoken but subtly shared, and slowly wafted away on the undulating reflections of the moonbeams bouncing off the rhythmic ocean waves below.

The moon was becoming hazy behind a film of silky clouds.

"Kiss me, Johnny."

He complied with tenderness and a keen awareness of how special this moment was, how special Grace was. The evening became indelibly etched in both their memories. It formed one cornerstone for what was to come.

Chapter 5 — Mysty Pages

OT MOLD?

"Holly, I swear you cringe every time we drive past that sign. Just do it!'"

"I know Bonny, I know. Sally's been harping on me about it too. It just seems so, I don't know, disruptive, disrespectful. Plus, they use all those toxic chemicals."

"Holly, mold is toxic too. So there is nothing disrespectful about annihilating it! And, as you move all the furniture around to get at the walls, you're likely to find many of the items you seem to have lost over the years," Bonny teased.

"I didn't mean disrespectful to the mold, Bonny. Screw the fungus. I meant disrespectful to Doug. He really tried his best to build us a weatherproof cottage on the dunes. How was he to know the foundation would sink so far into that sand?"

"My dear darlington Holly, Doug is probably spinning in his grave because you aren't dealing with his moldy walls!" She gave her friend a squeeze around the shoulders as they proceeded down Main Street.

Their turn was just past the postage-stamp-sized city park with the obligatory slice of an old growth tree bole sporting little interpretive arrows pointing at growth ring dates. Few paid enough attention to note that the arrow for Columbus landing was closer to the outside than the one for the Declaration of Independence, which in turn was closer than the one for the start of World War I. The rearrangement was an ineffectual high school prank and several arrows had since fallen off.

The Mysty Pages bookstore and coffee shop was not on the main drag of coastal Highway 101 and did not especially cater to tourists, except for frequent visitors in the know. Owner and operator Mary Duneflower Jackson liked it just fine that way. In-a-hurry tourists could get their coffees at the espresso drive-through stands found every other block on alternate sides of the highway as it passed through the main drag of town. SUV's and RV's didn't even have to cross lanes or turn around to get their quick fix. Mysty Pages catered to people who wanted to come and sit a while, discuss affairs of the day in a cozy fragrant setting, maybe waste half a day browsing through an unusual book, or read the Sunday Oregonian newspaper from cover to cover.

It was the perfect place for the weekly Saturday morning (meaning 10ish) meeting of the Mysty Pages Precipitation Society (Mypps for short).

"I'd say it's pissing a misty drizzle," Holly opined.

"Yep, I'd say you are right," Bonny concurred.

Just as Eskimos had developed several dozen words to describe different varieties of snow, Mypps specialized in defining terms for precipitation. Almost every Saturday for at least eight months of the year, the group would have a new variation to analyze and categorize over coffee at

Mysty Pages. Holly was actually compiling a book of definitions. Besides Holly Darlington and Bonny Sopp, several other cranberry farmers' wives routinely joined the discussion. It was a very unorganized and informal group. As for "pissing a misty drizzle," drizzle could soak through one's hair in half an hour, mist took about hour, and the precipitation today was intermediate. The pissing part referred to a gusty sea breeze that flung the moisture at a slant from the west, where Neptune often let loose. Whenever the day's description of precipitation had a misty component, they called it a concurrence day meaning it concurred with the name of Mary's combination bookstore/coffee shop.

"Whose rusted-out old Datsun pickup is that anyway? It's been blocking the prime parking spot for months now. Why doesn't Mary have it towed?"

Bonny, Holly reflected, obviously didn't understand the finer points of lawn ornamentation or landscape design. "Oh, it has character," she responded. "Besides, it adds to the milieu. Furthermore, it reminds me that we need to work on the scale for the salt content dimension of our PDM."

"Right!" Bonny scoffed. "Maybe we can predict how quickly this heap decomposes with our highfalutin' Precipitation Descriptor Matrix."

"Anyway," continued Holly, "I think Mary leaves it there because it prevents parking and unparking immediately in front of the shop. It does seem quieter and more serene inside of late."

"Hmmph, well I guess I agree with that, but it was probably just a way for one of Mary's many nephews to dispose of an old clunker."

That too, perhaps, Holly thought to herself.

"Concurrence day, ladies?" Mary guessed from behind the counter as they left the errant ray of sunlight striking the shrubbery outside and entered the toasty, humid, aroma-filled enclave.

"Concurrence day!" They echoed simultaneously as they leaned together in a forward crouch and pumped their right arms and fists in choreographed unison. Half of the purpose of Mypps (and the content of Holly's book-to-be) was the correspondence between precipitation types and Mary's coffee drinks. Her concurrence creations were everyone's favorites. They were all creations featuring different amounts of milk, sugar, and spices, as well as varied blending techniques, depending on the current precipitation droplet size, density, temperature, velocity, and wind direction.

"It's pissing a misty drizzle, Mary," Holly announced loudly. A few out-of-towners turned their heads, showing expressions of mild astonishment and amusement, but soon returned to their drinks and shifted their conversation to comments about local color.

"Got it!" and Mary turned to create two 2 percent lattes. The heavier the precipitation, the more milk fat she added. Mist was usually 1 percent, but the drizzle part jacked it up to 2 percent, the upper end for mist. She added a pinch of brown sugar to sweeten the dull day and bubbled the drinks with steam (the pissing part) to stir it all up. Bonny sprinkled a little cinnamon on hers to represent the rust on the Datsun parked outside.

They settled into their favorite nook in back. Mary

always seemed to have inventive ways of discreetly reserving it for them. It might be piles of books on the seats or a mop in a bucket left in the aisle. Sometimes it consisted of spills on the table that were not wiped up until they sat down. Usually Mary's tabby Freda just curled up in the middle of the bench and stared anyone else away until a member of Mypps brought her the requisite saucer of cream.

"Hi Freda," Holly cooed in a kitty voice. It's only a misty drizzle today, so I'm afraid its only 2 percent. OK?"

Freda yawned, feigning indifference, but lapped it up anyway, and then vacated her spot.

"Kinda quiet," Holly expounded at length.

"Yep," replied Bonny in kind. "Most of the cranberry farmers wives are busy helping with the harvest and processing right now. I only convinced Bugs to let me come today because I plied him with his favorite elk stew and rorsopp gravy last night."

"Whatsopp?"

"Rorsopp." It's Norwegian for the King bolete mushrooms I picked in the spruce forest last week."

"Jah, youse Norgies are real sopps for mushrooms," Holly jested. It was an old joke and Bonny ignored it. Unadventurous eaters would always suffer impoverished lives.

They didn't have a quorum to make decisions about components of the PDM, so they focused on savoring their drinks and the ambiance for a while. Shortly, Mary was able to take a break and join them.

"Hi girls. How's drips?"

"Wet," they further concurred.

Usually Mary's tabby Freda just curled up in the middle of the
bench and stared anyone else away until a member of Mypps
brought her the requisite saucer of cream.

The threesome of old friends eased into a relaxed conversation about nothing in particular as Freda peered around the corner of the planter and started eyeing the beacon of sunlight that now illuminated a spot on the cushion between Holly and Mary. The other customers had all left and they had the place to themselves.

While they quietly conversed, each noted the muted sounds of shuffling and footsteps upstairs.

"Grace?" Holly asked.

"Yeah," Mary confirmed. "She got into town last week. It sure has been nice having her around again. I didn't realize how much I had missed her."

"I know what you mean, Mary," Holly confided, "I feel the same way about Sally being back, although it was a real shame why she returned." The girls all knew that story; Holly had Bonny's and Mary's complete sympathy on Sally's behalf.

Soon a series of foot-stomps increased in volume as Grace descended the stairs that led from the upstairs residence into the adjacent bookstore. It seems boots were the preferred footwear of professional environmentalists. She was a veritable picture of youthful enthusiasm as she entered the coffee shop from the bookstore.

"Hi." she greeted them, as she tossed her silky black shoulder-length hair back and forth to get it off her collar. "What a stunning day!"

Well, Grace was right. It might have been pissing a misty drizzle on the way over, but a glorious sun was burning off all of the surface moisture in coiling streamers now, and the whole world seemed alive with possibility. Such were Mypps's challenges. No member ever claimed precipitation patterns were static.

"Hiya Grace," they each intoned in their own style. "Join us!"

"Only if mamaw will fix me my favorite black Moche mocha!" Grace asked with a statement.

Uppity child, Mary chuckled to herself as she went to do so.

Grace set aside her daypack and settled directly into the sunny spot next to Holly, much to Freda's exasperation. It was an old and amiable rivalry though, and soon Grace seduced Freda to sit on her lap in the sun.

"It's really nice to see you again Grace," Holly began. "Sally said the two of you have already gotten together a few days ago to do some reminiscing."

"Yes. Sally and I had a great time. Neither of us had been around here much for about seven years now. It is really fun to touch base again."

Both older women thought that "return home" might have been a better way to put it, but they kept that opinion to themselves.

"So Ole…" they both started at once, and then stopped in embarrassment.

Grace giggled and shook her head at them. "I think she likes him," she said.

Understatement was an art form among both Native Americans and Norwegians. Holly, who was neither, but whose concern was most salient, simply tried to abide the local norms.

Mary returned, "Here dearie." She sat pushing Grace closer to Holly and Bonny. The only disgruntled soul was Freda. The sunspot was now in the thigh valley between

Grace and Mary.

"I hear you came to town for a while on behalf of The Conservancy, Grace?" Bonnie asked tentatively. Neither she nor Bugs were rabid anti-environmentalists, but they did run a cranberry farm. Although it remained relatively profitable so far, market forces conspired to chip away at their income every year. Something had to change if they were to remain in business. Greater production and the CFA's JCBEP was the pat answer. Bugs and Bonnie had discussed Grace's professional mission with some trepidation, although they both liked her a lot.

"You bet," Grace replied with enthusiasm. "Those bog lands are special beyond belief. There has got to be a way to preserve them and help everyone else at the same time!"

Well, that sounded outright nebulous, Bonny thought. "How would one do that?" she nevertheless asked sincerely.

"Collaboration," Grace pronounced, as if it were a benediction.

Just as Bonny started to form a reply, the coffee shop door burst open and an unlikely visitant materialized.

It seemed to be a young man. His shoes were covered with drying mud, his jeans were sandy, and the limp hood of a vegetation-smudged jacket was pulled up over his head. Hours of misty drizzle had soaked his attire. Strands of wet black hair dangled out of the hood around his besmirched face. Waves of dishevelment seemed to waft from him.

"Johnny!" Grace bolted upright displacing table settings, spilling concurrence drinks, and sending Freda off like a terrified meteor.

The figure froze. Then it slowly turned to face them.

Mary was already on top of the situation. She calmly rose and approached the Johnny-specter.

"Hi," she said. "Welcome." She encouraged him to shed his sweatshirt and handed him a towel to dry his hair.

Grace, still standing, Holly and Bonny still sitting, were completely taken aback.

"What …what…" Grace started, but Johnny squinted at her with a distant look that cut her off abruptly.

Then his head slumped, and he asked meekly, "Can we talk Mary?"

Holly and Bonny found immediate excuses to depart. Bonny had to go help Bugs with the harvest anyway.

Grace lingered. "Johnny, you look like you've been dragged through a swamp. What's happened?"

"Nice to see you again too," he recovered a bit, "but…"

What's going on? She fretted.

"…well, excuse me Grace. I know it's been a long time, but I really need to talk to Mary right now. See you later?" His eyes beseeched them both.

"Sure," said Mary, "let me close up shop. It's slow anyway."

Grace just remained motionless and stared at Johnny. He finally met her gaze. They had not seen each other since she had gone off to college. The detritus of their abortive high school relationship hung like mobiles in the time and space between them.

"Johnny, its really good…" Grace started, but stopped when she saw the tenderness, longing and the old pain of rejection in his eyes

"Yeah," he said, then looked down to avoid her

intense gaze.

Mary returned and said, "Do you mind?" to Grace. "Johnny and I have been discussing tribal history of late, and I think he might have a lot on his mind."

Johnny blushed this time (red on red was not just an angry Indian) and glanced at Grace.

"Go for it," Grace said, "but Johnny, I'd love to spend some time with you soon. Catch up on old times?"

Johnny hesitated, but then straightened his shoulders and said simply, "Sure."

"Then how about the Puddle Inn for fish and chips tomorrow evening at seven?" Grace asked in her pert professional manner. "I hear Frog in a Bog is playing. They might not be professionals, but we always used to have fun dancing to them."

"Sure." he replied again, looking directly into her eyes again. Did she detect a bit more enthusiasm with the second 'Sure'?

"See you there then."

Grace thought he seemed more distracted than embarrassed, but left him and Mary to their tribal tales anyway. She loved such tales, but had already heard all of mamaw's stories many times over, or so she thought. Grace grabbed her backpack, with laptop inside, and left for the library where she could use their Wi-Fi to check her email without distractions. Johnny and Mary disappeared into the bookstore.

∫

Mary led Johnny to her private

space/office/study/meditation-chamber located through a discreet door, hidden behind a nondescript curtain, off an obscure isle, in the back of the bookstore. It was small, crammed with memorabilia and decorated with Native American artifacts and art work. Johnny felt overwhelmed, so he didn't even try to take it all in. Mary was one of the tribe's most revered elders, so examining her personal collection of important objects seemed like it would be an invasion of privacy. She took the comfortable lounger, and he sat upright in the wooden chair.

An hour later....

"Not bad" was all Mary Duneflower commented. "Have some coffee. Now I will tell you the history of the Sand Coast clans."

She paused, collected her sagacious thoughts, and continued, "This afternoon I will relate part of the tale of our people's disenfranchisement. Later, we will delve deeper in time and closer to the curse of the haunted bog from which you fortuitously emerged unscathed, though changed."

Johnny felt as if a great weight had been lifted from his chest. He had lost himself entirely in his story. Mary had not said a word. She had listened without judgment or reaction. Unburdening his thoughts and recent experiences had felt very liberating. In Elder Mary Duneflower Jackson he had found someone he could trust completely. Now he found himself listening intently to what she had to say.

"When white people first started showing up here in their big boats, our people started getting sick and dying. They shot and killed some of us too, mostly out of fear at first. We also shot some of them with our arrows. They acted so belligerent, greedy, and randy."

"You must have a general idea of our tribal history from the books I loaned you in prison. Skirmishes between natives and invaders started in 1851 at Battle Rock. By 1855, the Rogue Indian Wars engulfed the coast too. We were hunted by murderous bands of whites whose intent was to exterminate us. The fighting culminated when Tecumtum and his band surrendered in July, 1856 and were marched to a holding camp in Port Orford. There they were boarded, 600 at a time, onto the steamship Columbia and dispatched, very much against their will, to the newly established coastal reservation called the Siletz Agency. Some were taken to the Grand Ronde Reservation. Other south coast tribes, including ours, were forced to march to these places, sometimes through winter weather, over the dunes and rocky headlands. The small reservations became sequestering places for natives who still hindered the covetous settlers. Original clan or tribal affiliation meant little or nothing to our captors. All were concentrated in the same camps. By 1857, white settlers commenced ditching and draining our bogs to raise cattle and sheep to feed the gold miners, ship builders, and loggers."

"Later, other whites who were more educated talked to us and started writing down our names and tales on their leaves of paper. What they recorded about us inaccurately reflected our customs, culture, and ancestral lineages. Still, it contains important information that we otherwise might have lost."

"You know there had always been two peoples on the Sand Coast, as white folk call our homelands now: those who lived on the low swampy lands and coastal dunes, and others that lived in the upland hills and forests. Both were analyzed to be of Athapascan linguistic stock. This sounded to us like they were placing us into a herd of cows that grunted the same way. We could communicate. Did that mean we were the same people?"

"Anyway, the chroniclers and anthropologists always struggled with our languages, and transcribed them as best they could. Several spellings resulted. Those of us who originally lived among the low wetlands near the sea called ourselves the Quatomah, that is, the People of the Inside Water. Our tribal name was also spelled as Kwatami or Kwataime. We were the northern most villages of the Tututni tribal group."

"Those who lived predominantly in the hills surrounding us, and to the north were called the Mishikhuwutmetunne, that is, the People who live on the Stream called Mishi. The Mishi is now called the Coquille River."

"By 1885, the first cultivated cranberries were being planted where native bogs used to provide us with abundant fish, fowl, berries, and game. To do so, the white farmers ripped up all the native vegetation, shoveled the soil into rectangular ponds, and planted a cranberry native to eastern North America."

"Ironies abound. Our brothers and sisters in the east gave cranberries as gifts of peace or symbols of peace and friendship. The Thanksgiving holiday itself evolved from these feasts of peace. The other irony is that tribal members who avoided the march to Siletz, or who returned against all odds, were hired as marginal wage laborers to hand-pick the farmer's cranberries."

"To be sure, the farmers, their wives, and their children picked cranberries too. Look at this old photo. It shows a mixed group of whites and Indians, all ages and both genders, picking cranberries in 1916 near Bandon. The Indians got 50 cents a bushel in pay and might harvest three bushels a day. Fair pay at the time perhaps, but work was a new concept. Labor, for an overseer, supplanted subsistence livelihoods."

"My greatmamaw was pregnant when her people were forced to march north to the Siletz. She refused to go and was left behind with just a few other old women who were too feeble to walk so far. A settler family called Gorseman protected and provided for greatmamaw and her infant daughter, my grandmamaw, as the others were being marched north. The Gorseman family claimed the now vacant land where the lodges of our family's village were crumbling. Greatmamaw and grandmamaw—see the little girl—stand next to the two white women on the left side of this picture."

"The Gorsemans were decent folk, Johnny. So were the Sopps and most other settlers who became livestock and cranberry farmers. They had an appreciation for the earth and for a balanced human society. They simply had little appreciation for the native societies and ways of subsistence that existed previously in this place. How could they? They had left their own people. They felt the need to create their old sense of place in a new land."

"Other white immigrants were callous, rude, and even murderous. Such men disdained norms of behavior and considered themselves free to do anything they wanted. They scoured the land and streams to find nuggets of gold.

They cut and sold grandmother trees as if they owned them. They marked off pieces of the earth, and then they bought and sold these for unearned profit. They deceived and stole from each other, and from anyone else they could dupe."

"More to the point, Johnny, these lawless profiteers ripped off your tribe! You see, I have traced your family's history."

"WHAT?" Johnny started from his listening trance.

"Patience," she chided gently.

"You are actually a descendant of one of the chief families of the Mishikhuwutmetunne."

Johnny stared at her speechlessly for a moment. Then he asked, "How do you know that?"

"Two ways: first, because my greatmamaw never left her homeland. She collaborated with the few remaining older women from all the local tribes to share and to pass on the stories, traditions and family lineages that they remembered as best they could. My own mamaw died when I was six years old and she had not been interested in our traditions anyway. So my grandmamaw raised me. Greatmamaw had taught the old ways to my grandmamaw, who then passed them on directly to me."

"But," Mary continued emphatically, "It is important to note that our people who did trek north to the Siletz Agency and Grand Ronde Reservation did not entirely abandon their tales or traditions either."

"Do you remember returning here with your mother?" Mary asked gently.

Johnny thought about it. The memory was vague, like a movie watched long ago.

"Your mother might have been a drunk when she brought you back from Siletz, but I extracted a lot of information from her before she handed you off to Aunt Jenny. You are descended from a head family of the nearby southern foothill clan of the Mishikhuwutmetunne. Your ancestral lands have been mined, logged, grazed, sold, and developed. Do you know the Latterly family?"

Johnny squirmed.

∫

The next evening, Grace shouted, "Yo! Johnny!" across the Puddle Inn parking lot as he climbed out of the Datsun pickup he had borrowed from Mary.

"Hi Gracie," Johnny said softly and affectionately as he slowly approached and checked her out.

They just stood and looked at each other for a few moments. "Mutually awkward" would be an appropriate understatement.

"Inside?" Grace leaned, pointed, and smiled. "Sure." Johnny brightened a bit.

Neither had been in the Puddle Inn since before they had been old enough to drink booze legally. Regardless, both had often invaded the Puddle during their high school years to dance and party. It was the only scene in town. Grace mostly abstained, but boogied. Johnny had broken the rules and partied hearty. They now returned in an entirely new context and each was wary of what the other was thinking.

"I love fish and chips," Grace informed the waitress. "Bring them on. Give me a triple serving of fish!"

Johnny said, "A big salad, and a large portion of baked flounder please. Maybe some steamed broccoli too."

Grace's astonished look elicited a feigned innocent response from Johnny. "What?" Then they both broke out in guffaws.

"Drinks?" The bored waitress inquired, not even fazed.

"Iced tea, please." said Sally.

"A root beer," said Johnny.

The waitress glanced up from under her long fake eyelashes and then around the boisterous bar. "No root beer," she said.

Johnny twitched his lips to indicate thinking and looked aside to hide evidence of his mischievousness. "How about a pitcher of milk then?"

The waitress tilted her head down and to the right, cranked her eyeballs up and to the left, and looked straight at Johnny with a withering gaze.

"Just teasing," he continued blandly. "How about a glass of ice water and a decaf after dinner?"

She departed quickly. Drunks were bad enough. Oh, how she wished she could get promoted to the family restaurant side of the Puddle!

Over dinner, they caught up with each other. Grace refrained from expounding upon her accomplishments in college and her new career. Johnny did not dwell upon his incarceration, subsequent quest for identity, or attempt at a vision quest. The lack of details didn't matter. They knew they would have some time to catch up while she was in town on assignment for the bog conservation project. Anyway, they both had been asking others about each other.

"Care to dance, Johnny?"

It had been a long time, he thought, not so much in years, but in dreams.

"You bet."

Chapter 6 — Love Yearns

"Your desire twists your judgment, Love Flames! The land is moist. If the fire burns too lightly this time, then it will be hard to light again for several years because the little fire-food will be gone. When we do get it to burn again, there will be too much large fire-food and the fire will grow so hot that it will kill many of the berry bushes."

Love Flames did itch to light the fire. He always did. He lived for fire ever since he aggressively played with campfire brands as a toddler. However, he was certain he was right, too. "No, little brother," he said as he sniffed the wind, felt the breeze and snapped a few more twigs, "you are wrong. Now is exactly the best time to light the fire."

"The rain last week did dampen the woods and brush, but the steady wind this week has sucked out most of that wetness. It also has been a dry summer, so that all this land was already parched before the rain. We should not wait because it has already been too many years since we last burned this area. Look, those dark clouds racing at us from the south end of the sea are filled with rain that will not stop again until next summer."

"Losing our chance to burn this year," he continued,

"is not the most important reason though. You can feel the wind stiffen in front of that looming storm even now. If we light the fire this moment, those winds will push the flames rapidly through this whole area. Embers will hop ahead like frogs in a race. The bushes and trees will be burned just enough so that next year there will be berries in great abundance, but the rain that follows the wind will put out the fire before too much burns. Trust me! We start the fire right now!"

Love Flames squatted and twirled his drill stick against the flat piece of notched wood. Within seconds, he had a smoking ember, and in less time than it would take for three slow breaths, he had flames licking through his bundle of cattail fluff and crumbly moss. He set his brother's pitchy torch afire and then his own. They headed out in opposite directions, sideways to the wind direction, setting the brush and grasses alight as they ran from spot to spot. The wind suddenly increased in strength and gustiness. The flames leapt from bush to bush and raced through the grasses, shrubs and pines. The sky rapidly filled with smoke downwind to match the storm clouds upwind. Reaching the river, he paused and watched for several minutes. The fire was a raging monster; this was Love Flames' favorite part. Tall flames licked through the dancing columns of smoke. Sparks and embers flew on the wind and traced trails of glowing red through the brown murkiness.

He startled from his revelry, as an unnerving wail of despair suddenly split the gathering darkness. It had come from in front of his wall of flames. NO! Please, Great Mystery, please, let it not be so!

Love Flames was a hunter and warrior of his hills tribe. He did not hesitate to kill for good reason, but he always dreaded a person being trapped in the path of his flames. It had never happened before. Let it not be so now!

"What was that?" panted his brother as he came running back to his side. Love Flames' look of alarm was ample answer.

The brothers had worn their fire sandals made from three layers of thick elk hide wrapped high on their calves. Both also wore leather britches and had brought along woven masks that could be stuffed with wetted moss and strapped over their mouths and nostrils if the wind shifted and the smoke became troublesome. They quickly dunked in the river to wet all their clothing and then strapped on the masks. "This way," Love Flames urged, and took off through the smoke and flames, winding his way through the smoldering bushes and hot spots. He had been closest to the wail and had the best sense of its direction. Large raindrops began to fall, sizzling and hissing as they struck hot embers.

They dreaded what they would find. Although hunting and gathering areas overlapped, his tribe typically kept to the hills and the dunes tribes kept to these inside waters and the coast. There were plenty of deer, elk, fish, berries and other resources to go around, so the two neighboring tribes simply traded for special goods like coastal shellfish or foothill acorns. The dunes tribes did not have much experience with lighting land fires though, so his tribe often restored these border berry bogs as a trade favor. He had personally informed the dunes chief that they might try to light a fire today. Let there not be a victim!

"Yai!, Yai!" Love Flames yelled in hope of a response whenever he could catch his breath. The flames were sputtering out as the rain hardened, but the air was still dense with soot-filled vapors and steam. The day was not quite done, but the fumes, black clouds, and burned branches conspired to create a surreal world, one filled with dark sinister shapes that glowed a dull red in the wavering light of flickering flames. The brothers stuck close together in their desperate search.

"That forest is still burning too hot. Besides, I think the wail was from this direction," Love Flames guessed, as they groped away from an impenetrable wall of fire. Soon though, they found their path blocked by a small lake, edged with bog and swamp plants. Cornered by river, flames, and lake, they could go no further.

"Aiiiiii!" Little brother's blood-curdling screech of terror rent the moment. Jumping loosely in his skin, Love Flames twisted to see what had so frightened his partner in fire. The young man stood like a rigid totem pole, shock on his distorted face, his arm stiffened, shaking, and pointing at the lake. There, at the lake's edge, was a spectral form rising from the water and muck. It was covered in bog weeds, dripping muddy streams, and struggling toward them like one of the dead. A lightening bolt split the sky and lit the scene with startling clarity. It was a ghastly young maiden. With one hand she reached to grasp them. In the other, she held what looked like two arrows, one for each of their hearts! She slowly lifted her head and gazed at them with baleful eyes.

"KA-Rack!" the thunder covered her first cough. Her

There, at the lake's edge, was a spectral form rising from the water and muck.

next coughs blended with the rumbling aftermath to produce a sound like a beast gagging on blood. Little brother unfroze and bolted, but Love Flames was rooted to the spot. Then she collapsed at the water's edge and coughed some more. The tableau was shattered, the illusion broken. Love Flames ran to help her. She was shivering uncontrollably from the cold water.

∫

"You slimy bogman, see where your wisdom has led us!" accused the old woman as she threw a putrid clam at him. Beyond Old Gull tried to ignore her, but as he continued to shuffle along, little children came up to strike his shins with sticks. He swept his ancient yew staff just above their heads and growled "UUrrgghah!" at them with the greatest nastiness he could muster from his failing voice, but they only scattered for a few moments. Many derisive stares were directed toward him as he passed the other villagers on the way to his hut. They were probably speaking loudly about him, or to him, but he didn't need to hear their words to know their meaning. Indeed, his very name, Beyond Old Gull, so revered by many generations before, had been shortened and corrupted to the derogatory word, 'bog.' The same word was used for the stinking, bug-infested wetlands he had insisted they inhabit.

Long Gull (as he liked to think of himself) had hoped to at least avoid the chief today. It was not to be. As he rounded the front of the tribal lodge, Mountain Whale emerged and blocked Long Gull's path with his bulk and an aggravated stare. Mountain Whale, he had often reflected,

was named better than most. At least no one in the Far
Wanderers tribe could complain that his advice had led to
food shortages. They were getting fat and lazy, he scoffed
to himself, as he halted in front of the blubber mountain.

"We need to talk."

The sun shines, water is wet, Long Gull thought to
himself.

"Come, we walk."

Why in the endless seasons of time couldn't they just
sit down and talk, chafed Long Gull. At least Whales can't
walk very fast.

Mountain Whale left the village on the high firm path
that overlooked the sea, but which ended abruptly at a new
cutbank where the river now flowed across last year's trail.
He stopped at the edge, stood up straight, squared his
shoulders, spread his arms, and reveled in the brisk chill
ocean breeze. Skinny old Long Gull shivered with cold. The
mountain turned and looked at him without pity.

"See that otter below in this new-path river? My great
grandmother told me tales of your greatness when I was no
bigger than it." Long Gull remembered better than the
chief, but said nothing. "She said that you led our people
on a long journey, trudging for many generations from a
distant shore. How can that be old man? Do you never
die?"

"Tell me also, what happened to your wisdom? Has it
fled like a summer day? We had a rich and beautiful place
to live when I was young. No one bothered us. Shore rocks
covered with endless shellfish were only a stone's throw
away from our village. Our dwellings were on high land, but
sheltered by trees. Clean water flowed just below us in the

small stream that never dried up, rarely flooded, and was easy to cross. The forests, meadows, and streams were full of game, birds and fish. We had no need to brave the sea waves. Every year or two, one of the great ones would die on our long beach and everyone would have plenty of oil.

"Tell me again why you counseled us to move! Tell me again why you strove so hard to convince me!"

Long Gull cringed because the truth could not be told without incurring expulsion and exile. He tried to picture the Mountain's wrath if he attempted to explain his need. He could no longer live without the support of the tribe. He had become too feeble to explore far independently. He felt in his ancient bones, however, that the rot- and ground-fleshes that he needed were very near. He had found young stands of the pure-heart cedar and familiar oaks growing near this village site. He must find his deliverance here! What more could he tell this man mountain?

He drew himself up, suppressed his shivering, mustered all his remaining dignity, and stared Mountain Whale directly in the eyes.

Young fat pup, he thought.

He said, "Our tribe has many children. We do not fight or strive against our neighbors. We have food in abundance. Our young know their great-grandparents and our traditions fill many months of telling in the dark winter months. These are blessings you have always known, so you value them like water, which is everywhere. Our ancestors suffered, struggled, and died to get here. I counseled and taught them through good times and bad. I know better than any of you that wellbeing comes and goes in cycles that cannot be foretold, and that time eats all things.

"No! Wait! Hear me out! It does not matter how I know these things or how I have lived so long. Not to you or anyone else. These secrets are mine alone. What matters to you and the people is that if I die, you will lose a source of long wisdom that no other tribe possesses. You cannot deny the richness of our traditions. You cannot deny my ability to heal. You cannot deny that my foresight and wisdom have brought us around the rim of the sea, as your great-grandmother related in winter tales. Would you cut down the greatest tree because it dropped a few bothersome cones on your lodge roof? I needed this move. In the long future, the tribe will greatly benefit from this move. Our current circumstances are a small and temporary inconvenience. Better times will come. That is again my counsel."

"Greatest Tree! Counsel? Hah! You have become like the rot-flesh that eats the oldest stump! Your wisdom is like half-salty water that never flows and becomes covered with scum! You counseled us to move to a land of empty sand. 'Build the village up on top of that empty dune,' you said. No rocks with shellfish are within half a day's walk. The wind blows constantly and we lack natural shelter from it. We must walk further inland to hunt deer and elk, but then we encounter other tribes. Small birds inhabit the swamps and bogs, but it takes more patience to hunt them than the honking flocks that came to meadows where we last dwelt. Worst of all, the river where we now dwell wanders back and forth every winter like the kelp that children play with as whips. Of course we are not starving. That does not explain why you counseled us so urgently to move here. We should have stayed where life was even easier and richer. I cannot keep our tribe content. They remember better times. Other tribes now dwell where our lodges once stood. We will have to fight to return, but every family wishes to leave these shifting dunes. If you continue to insist we stay, you will soon be cast out. Heed my words."

The mountain of whale blubber staggered down the dune, heedlessly knocking Long Gull down into the soft sand as it passed. Way Beyond Old Long Gull had loved his tribe throughout his many lives, but was losing his tolerance and patience. They were becoming a selfish, discontented, and sluggish lot. Life was too bountiful here on the edge of the sunset water. Any inconvenience became a trial. Tradition counted for little in this new land. The people thought only of the immediate now, rather than the collection of nows that formed each of their lives and that of the tribe's long history.

Long Gull nursed growing resentment as he hobbled back through another demonstration of the tribe's disrespect.

$$\int$$

Love Flames felt no overt hostility from the tribe, but all their eyes were intent upon him. He sensed that most of them reserved judgment. Still, he was in their strange lodge, surrounded by their powerful sea-totems, transfixed by their gazes, and accountable to their judgment.

"Tell us your story." the massive chief proclaimed from his high huge seat at the far end of the lodge. He shifted his weight and grunted.

Love Flames chose to stand. He wanted all to see him. He wanted all to hear him clearly. He wanted all to know he felt no guilt. He spoke plainly in the common tongue.

"Two days before my brother and I started the fire, I came to this village. You know that. Many of you saw me here. I entered this lodge and spoke to your chief." He glanced at Mountain Whale, but the chief showed no sign of acknowledgment, so he continued.

"I told Whale Mountain that my brother and I planned to burn the berry bog lands in the next day or two. Our intent was to improve the berry picking and hunting for both our tribes in the coming years."

Love Flames stopped there. He had said what he had done. It was not his place to say what their chief had said or done. He sat down.

"What about Waits for Love?" asked the chief.

This was awkward. Should he stand again and further proclaim his truth? It might seem like he was being brazen. Or, should he reply while remaining seated, and thereby risk showing disregard or disrespect?

Love Flames cared deeply, so he slowly stood. He looked around at the gathered tribe. He lowered his head as if to compose his thoughts, and then lifted it and faced them. He spoke softly out of respect, but clearly. The assembly had to stop talking amongst themselves for most to hear. "Waits for Love, as I have come to know her name," he paused dramatically, "was brave and resourceful. Few warriors that I know would think to breath through reeds while hiding under a lake to escape flames. I did not save her. She saved herself. I regret my actions put her in peril."

It was as if the thrust of his praise for Waits, using the sharp bone of his admission to culpability, punctured the bloated seal bladder of uncertainty to let out the fetid gases of festering distrust. Everyone started talking at once, Mountain Whale gestured for food.

When Love Flames glanced at Waits for Love, she was beaming at him with a grateful smile.

He immodestly winked at her, utterly infatuated. Several older women, younger women, and non-betrothed younger men noticed. One man seethed with hatred. The rest paid no attention and started to eat.

Long Gull watched the drama without comment. The tribe seemed to welcome this fire-happy, love-struck outsider called Love Flames more than they did him. That mattered little. What did matter was that Love Flames had set fire to the very area he had thought most likely to harbor the rot- and ground-fleshes that he needed. He was not ready to call Love Flames a fool or to curse him. This practice of burning must have been going on for ages; but what if this young fire lover had delayed or ruined his chances? Both fleshes seemed to depend on particular trees. Tomorrow he would suck on many mouthfuls of pounded willow bark and drag his stiff aching bones back across the dunes to the small lake where he had found the pure heart cedars and rare oaks. He had to know.

∫

"Come Wave Eyes, I want to show you something." It was very early on a misty summer morning. Most were sleeping past daybreak because the days were so long now that one had to sleep during some of the daylight, and it might as well be in the morning. Long Gull had quietly pulled the child from next to his older sister, Waits for Love, without her or anyone else noticing. The boy only slowly awoke as they left the village and he put Wave Eyes down to walk by himself. They were evenly paced. Long Gull hobbled and Wave Eyes tottered along on stubby legs, not knowing where they were going or what was happening. Before long, he lifted Wave Eyes into a canoe and paddled up the low languid river. Wave Eyes fell soundly asleep again on dry moss piled on the bottom of the canoe.

When Wave Eyes awoke, he found himself in a very strange place. There was a small lake with odd water plants all around the shore. The bogman was sitting a little ways off, on the edge of the lake. At the man's back, there were many small strange trees. They grew in a clump and together the treetops were rounded, like the ground-fleshes that poked out of the sand when it rained. The trees had dark brown hair on their branches. Wave Eyes stumbled over to the old man, rubbing his eyes.

"Hello nephew," the bogman said, "here, have some salmon and water. You must be hungry and thirsty." Wave Eyes was both. He ate, drank, and relieved himself by one of the flat leaved trees. He didn't know where he was, so he could only return to the old man. He sat next to him and looked at him with curiosity. Fear or peril had not entered his mind. The day was warming.

"Let me tell you a story," began the bogman. As with every jump, it proved useful to tell the lad the tale of his long life. Comprehension mattered little. Such young minds could not be expected to understand and the boy would be unable to explain his secrets. He was simply preparing a proper bed for his own mind. Once he jumped, the assimilation was smoother and more complete.

So nephew Wave Eyes listened to the old man drone on; the voice made him sleepy again. Uncomprehending, he soaked up the tale like tree beards suck up water when it rains.

"You are a part of my ancient lineage. The whole tribe is. I have mated with nearly all of its generations. Your mothers and fathers, brothers and sisters, aunts and uncles, and cousins are all my direct or indirect offspring. I am the tribe, as no other is. In early years, some of our children had misshapen bodies or were ill at birth. We set them adrift in the sea in small ceremonial canoes, asking the Great Mystery that our tribe's imbalance be cleansed. Eventually, it was. Our breeding is now true and wholesome.

"You are the youngest and best scion of our tribe. You will be me. I will be you. I have at last found the way. It is here, in this grove. You cannot see it now, but I found the decaying remains this last winter. Meanwhile, look at these strange shelves of hard rot-flesh, the ones growing out of the ancient pure-heart cedars around the lake, the ones with the blunt fingers underneath. They will let me live for four more moons until the next season of retreating sun, advancing rain, and awakened ground-fleshes.

"Then you and I will come here again. We will be one. We will live forever!" Wave Eyes still did not understand, but it did not sound like something he wanted to do. He wanted to go back to his sister Waits for Love. Eventually they did, and his sister was very mad at the bogman.

∫

The boggy lake where he had first met Waits for Love amid the dying flames was now Love Flames' favorite place to linger and think. He came here to dwell on how to win her as his mate. Was it possible? Their tribes were so different. Yet, he desired her with a depth of emotion that seemed to transcend time. He knew she longed for him too, if only from her grateful gaze as he drew her from the lake, from the way she lingered in his embrace after she had warmed up in his arms, from the intense glances they had shared in the chief's lodge. How could two people yearn so strongly for each other and remain apart?

The days were starting to grow longer. Soon the sun would shine more warmly. He would find a way to court her as the people wandered from their lodges seeking fresh foods. He would give her many flowers. Love Flames now loved Waits more than flames.

One day, as he sat next to the lake, planning his courtship, the dune tribe's old shaman and a very young boy had appeared out of the morning fog. He thought he recognized the boy as Waits for Love's younger brother. Love Flames had excellent hearing. He remained silent and immobile downwind behind a bush as the old man talked to the boy for half the morning. Although he struggled to understand, he overheard most of what the bogman said. What did he mean, "being one?" The shaman had hinted at immortality too. Could love be unending as well?

Chapter 7 — My Land

"Do you really think there is going to be violence, sheriff?"

Ray Wilson sat back in his chair, closed his eyes, and composed himself briefly before responding. He could see her in his mind's eye. Just barely eighteen, pudgy, trying to fit into a dress she had outgrown since last wearing it, spray-encrusted brown hair curled up on both sides in an out-of-date 60s style, shifting nervously from foot to foot as she fiddled with a notepad and chewed on a wooden pencil. What did they teach kids in high school journalism class nowadays?

"I did ... not ... say that," Sheriff Ray responded emphatically and with as much patience as he could muster. "I said that it is my job to ensure that my staff is prepared for all contingencies."

She scribbled something hastily, and skewered him with her eyes again. "Then why are ALL the deputies on duty today?" she prompted. "How many does it take to, and I quote, 'prepare for all contingencies,' unquote."

Ray groaned at her asinine flourish of trite formal language. "Just what makes you think they are?" he countered.

"Sheriff, you are not forgetting who I am, are you? I know everything in this town. Before it happens."

Ray certainly knew who Maybelle Tattleton was, or more to the point, her skills and network.

"Look, Maybelle, I know you are the Berry Queen, I know you are the town gossip, and I know you are covering this meeting for your journalism class project. None of that gives you the privilege to put words in the mouths of public officials!" he spat, patience wearing thin. He had more important things to do just now.

She eyed him carefully, trying to decide what to read into his demeanor. "So, let's see, 'County Sheriff Rattled Even Before Contentious Land Use Meeting,' how's that for a headline?"

Ray spun in his chair and gave her his very best impatient officious eye. "If you want a story," he almost growled in his frustration, "just go to the meeting and report what happens! That's news! That's investigative journalism! You are demeaning yourself by wallowing in tabloid sensationalism based on misquoting busy public safety officers! Get OUT!" Ray turned around, ignoring and dismissing her, and picked up his phone.

"Maybe 'Preparing For Violence, Sheriff Evicts Journalist'?"

"OUT!" He flew to his feet, towered over her, and pointed to the door.

"County Sheriff Suffers Stroke During Interview," she scribbled on her notepad while stumbling down the front stairs in her awkward and unfamiliar heels. She glanced around and then headed off to pursue other leads. She might be able to corral some arriving deputies out back.

Several were friends of the family.

Ray collapsed in his chair and sighed. The worst part was, Maybelle was onto the truth. He was expecting trouble. He had never before seen an issue divide the community like these twin development proposals. Everyone had a fervent opinion on both and many meant to speak their minds tonight. Knowing some of the bull-headed citizens of this town and surrounding countryside, arguments were likely to get heated. Calm negotiation of mutually beneficial solutions was not a local skill.

Ray had even called the high school superintendent Bob Wilkins last week. "Hi Bob" etc., small talk ... "Say Bob, there aren't any problems with the school gym or repairs that might be needed. Just want to make sure it is safe for the meeting. We could always ask the Lutheran church to hold the meeting in their auditorium. My wife is the secretary there," he hinted.

The Lutheran church auditorium was smaller, so would hold fewer hotheads. Ray also hoped the religious setting might engender a more respectful debate.

Bob didn't get the hint. Bob was very literal minded and didn't even suspect hidden meaning in Ray's query. "Why gosh, no, Ray. No problems at all. You know we had a fire inspection only last month and the school sponsors regular safety drills. The GOT MOLD guys even got around to repainting the women's bathroom walls a couple of weeks ago. We're good to go with the meeting!" Bob enthused to Ray's disappointment.

"OK, thanks Bob, just checking. See ya tonight."

"Sure," responded Bob, sounding puzzled. Best to just drop it there, Ray figured. If he explained more to Bob,

Maybelle would probably be all over the reasons for a change of venue like the first gull discovering an overturned truckload of Twinkies.

His head deputy chose that moment to come blustering in with an air of anticipation and excitement.

"Tasers?" he asked excitedly.

Ray groaned again, slumped in his chair, raised his hand to his forehead, and shook his head in disbelief. "God, NO, Billy, we are NOT going to carry our tasers tonight! These are citizens, not hardened criminals. What do you want to do, kill an upstanding farmer that happens to have a pacemaker? Watch soccer moms writhe on the linoleum? Put bake sale grandmas in the hospital? What's gotten into you?"

Looking chagrined, but unsatisfied, Billy pressed on. "Ray, we got that fat Homeland Security grant to buy special crowd control weapons, and we ain't never even had a chance to wear them! We don't have to use them, but maybe we should get some real live practice at carrying them, eh?"

Ray was already worn out, and the day was only half over. The real fun wouldn't start for several more hours. What next, he wondered? Water cannons? Tear gas? "No," he said simply but clearly, "go suit up normally and round up the other deputies. We're going to have a little chit-chat before tonight's deployment."

∫

Don's Chevron had the cheapest gas and best homemade Jo Jo's for 50 miles up and down 101.

Whenever they came to town, most locals stopped by to fill up, eat, obtain some convenience, or chat. This afternoon, the parade of motorists kept Donald Kirkpatrick hopping faster than a leprechaun. Both Don and Bugsy had visited their "ancestral homelands" in the previous year, and they savored every opportunity to practice their old country accents. Don had more opportunities at the gas station than Bugsy did on his cranberry farm, but they both bugged the heck out of their friends and neighbors with their affected lilts or ümlauts, as the case may be. Don felt "dis wuld be ai fyne day fer practicin' his hoppin n' yarnin'!"

In rapid succession, Sheriff Ray, several deputies, Ole, Wally, Bugs, Stan, Mary and Maybelle pulled in to fill up. Were they all topping off their tanks because they planned to boogie out of town immediately after the big meeting?

First, the county's newest patrol rig, a white 2016 Jeep Patriot with a new Arjent S2 lightbar sporting ultra bright white LED takedown lights, pulled slowly to the forward pump.

"Hiya sheriff. What kin I do ye fer?"

"Don," Ray nodded, as he removed his sunglasses, "top it off please. Would you take a gander at the tires while you're at it?"

"Sure Ray; preparing to chase rowdy citizens, eh?" Don hopped to it without another word when he saw the sheriff's expression.

Next came Ray's previous patrol vehicle, the white 2010 Jeep Grand Cherokee with the discontinued model Arjent SL LED lightbar.

"Hiya, Billy, what's the sheriff on 'bout?"

Billy Anders pouted and replied. "Ahh, he never let's

us carry our new tasers."

Don didn't want to touch that comment with a pike-pole, so he proceeded to top off the tank.

Second Deputy Tom Wards pulled in behind Billy with the rest of the assistant deputies. They were all piled in a dark blue 2008 Ford Explorer all wheel drive V8 sporting a Whelen Strobe/Halogen 9M lightbar.

"Hiya Tom, Chad, Frank, Warren," as he nodded to each of them in turn. "Planning on some long distance, high-speed chases tonight?" Don couldn't help himself. He was impishly Irish after all.

"What?" Tom seemed distracted with a business card. Don just got a glance at some lettering on it. "Journalist at … " something or other. It looked like an amateur had designed it: garish colors, poor contrast, weird font, and small lettering. Don's wife Ann ran a graphic design business in Port Orford; it occasionally invaded his TV time so he had a few clues about design errors.

"A … just fill it up Don." said Tom as he returned his attention to the moment and pocketed the card.

"OKee dokee." Don obeyed.

Ole's midnight blue 1997 Ford pickup truck pulled up to the diesel pump as Tom was signing the county's tab, so Don moved right along. Ole had popped the hood to check something and Sally was washing the back window and rear lights, waiting for Ole to lower the hood before she cleaned the windshield and headlamps.

"Hiya Ole. Mother Mary's smile, its nice te see ye agin Sal!"

"Hey Don, 'sup?" replied Ole, oblivious.

Sally was slightly taken aback by the liveliness of Don's

comment. "Howdy Don," she replied demurely.

"Ready fer de big meetin' tonight, Ole? I reckon the county's finest are preparing fer a big chase after."

"Huh?" was all Ole could think to respond. He knew Don never followed up his cryptic remarks with clarification, so he didn't even try.

"You coming, Don?" Sally asked.

"Would nay miss it fer de wurld, missie," he said, "I even dusted off me ol' boxin' gloves."

He winked at Sally as they drove away and he fancied to himself that she noticed as she glanced at him in the side mirror. He figured it was a married man's prerogative to flirt a little, as long as it was all in good fun. That Ole was a lucky guy!

Officious tribal head Wally One-Path Jackson pulled up next in his imposing jet black 2016 GMC Yukon XL Denali. Don didn't mind huge rigs with feet-per-gallon mileage. They just provided more business for him.

"Yo Wally!" Don teased.

Wally frowned at Don's disrespect and struggled to climb down out of the high seat in a dignified manner. Wally always watched pump attendants to make sure they didn't overfill the tank and spill gas on the side-panel paint. He would rather pump the gas himself, just to make sure, but a ridiculous Oregon law didn't allow self-service. Just wait. They would soon have their own filling station on their own sovereign tribal lands. Then Oregon laws be damned!

"Fillerup, Don, but stop pumpin' at the first click-off. I don't want no gas dribbling out."

"Rightoe, Wally-boy!" Don jibed him gleefully. He had

heard the admonition a hundred times before, but tweaking Wally's sense of self-importance was always entertaining.

Wally was getting better at ignoring him, so Don continued, "Think ye'll get permission from de powers dat be te build yer casino?"

"Don't need no permission from state or federal bigwigs, Don. Already got their sign-off. We just need to convince this shortsighted community its good for them too. You'd think they liked paying property taxes!" Wally winced as Don dramatically posed a gas-soaked rag under the nozzle, ready to wipe.

Returning a few small bills from the C-note, Don just said, "Gaed luck tenight."

Wally nodded, ascended his seat, settled in, and pulled away.

Before Don could take a break, Bugsy Sopp, Bob Newall, and Jake Booley pulled up in the CFA's tour vehicle. It was a new custom-color cranberry red 2016 GMC AWD Savana Passenger Van, perfect for navigating muddy berms while providing a comfortable ride to their city visitors. The CFA spared no expense wooing site inspection regulatory officials about their plans. In fact, there were going to be some honchos at this meeting. They wanted to be able to offer rides if such representatives felt like chatting more over drinks at Puddle Inn afterwards. Public servants were known to worry about driving government vehicles back to their motel while inebriated, let alone parking the vehicles near a tavern.

"Heya Bugs, how's boginess?"

"Vet," Bugs replied.

"What'll ye have?" Don asked.

Bugs looked at him wistfully. "Oh, I don' know, vat about profit, prosperity, bigger bogs, vurk fur de local volk? Is dat too much ta ask?"

"I pump gas, but we got some hot dinger Jo Jo's inside, Bugs." Actually, Bob and Jake hopped out and got some. It might be a long hungry meeting.

As the van pulled away, up drove Stan in his lustrous 2016 forest green BMW X5 xDrive35d turbo-diesel SAV (Sports Activity Vehicle). Prominently displayed on the back bumper was a red, white, and blue sticker reading, "100% Biodiesel. No Global Warming, No Blood for Oil, $ for US Farmers." Just let those damn greenie-weenies question the environmental rectitude of his land developments. He had used his vehicle as a devastating (or so he imagined) counter-argument more than once. Stan pulled up to the same fossil fuel diesel pump Ole had used.

"Hiya Stan, forget te fill up from yer barrel of home-delivered biodiesel again? If'n it be empty, I ken arrange another delivery." Both of them knew Stan rarely used it. It had been a year since the last such pretentious delivery. Pumping fuel was beneath Stan. That's what he paid Don to do.

"When are you going to zip your lips and get biodiesel here, Don? It's the wave of the future," he said without caring. Image was money, and he was just grooming his image, even if Don saw right through him.

"Fill it up?" Don inquired.

"What else?" Stan snapped back. Hmmm, a little testy, Don ruminated as he topped the tank.

Stanley C. Latterly just wanted this one last big deal to go through. He could pay off his house on the lake and retire in the lifestyle to which he had become accustomed. All he really needed was another 700 grand or so from this career capstone of a lucrative tribal casino deal. Tonight he hoped to sew up the loose ends. For instance, he hoped to deal with that Preservancy bullrot. Who are they to tell me what I can do with "my land," he fumed. Well, in this case, not exactly "my land" but land I am under comprehensive contract to develop!

"That'll be a whoopin' ten bucks, Stan." Don waited with curious anticipation.

Stan handed him a twenty and said, "You know what to tell Maybelle," and drove away without waiting for change. Don just shrugged and pocketed ten in change. Stan's bribes were so silly, but they did add up over time....

Mary Duneflower Jackson navigated the coughing rusted skeletal Datsun pickup to the next pump and jerked to a halt. As she put it out of its misery, the ferrous oxide-coated heap dieseled several times, discharged a black puff from its tail pipe, shuttered with a dramatic flourish as it died, and left a layer of reddish dust on the concrete underneath it. The door was small anyway, and she had parked so close to the pump it could only be opened part way. Smiling, as if she had a new toy, Mary struggled to get up out of the low seat and climb through the narrow gap.

"Hey Don!" Mary beamed before he could even get in a word. "Fabulous day, eh?" Mary was definitely one of Don's favorite customers, people for that matter. She was invariably upbeat on even the dreariest day, and always interested in him, his wife, and his business.

"How's Annie? I haven't seen her in the bookstore for a couple of weeks. Did she see Doc Willis again?"

"Annie's fine, Mary. Thanks fer askin'. She's jes a wee bit under de weather. Business hain't been very graphic lately."

"Tell her Hi, Don. I'm thinking about having her design a new sign for Mysty Pages. Something with more concurrence. If she can stop by for Mypps next Saturday, I'd love to chat with her about it. The society might want to provide some input into the design too."

"Will do. Headed fer de big shindig tonight?"

"Wouldn't miss it for the world, Don. I guarantee you tonight will be discussed for years to come. Happenings this evening will be deeply seminal!"

"Mary Dune, det's sounding vaguely pornographic! Mind if I quote ye te Maybelle?" who just happened to be pulling up to a pump at the other island.

"Tell Maybelle to go home and get her pop's old cassette tape recorder, Don, she won't be able to take notes fast enough tonight," she joked. She also paid, climbed back in the Datsun, and got it resurrected to noisy and noxious life before Maybelle could corral her.

"Bye Donny boy," she shouted out the window and waved as the rust bucket sputtered and lunged away.

Maybelle Tattleton had gotten her driver's license shortly after becoming the Berry Queen. Her father, fearing the combination was too heady for an eighteen year-old, only let Maybelle drive the recently replaced, previous family vehicle. It was a boxy, dull tan, 1988 Nissan Stanza wagon with moldy carpet and worn seats. GOT MOLD had not diversified into cars, although they periodically thought about it during economic downturns. Anyway, most folk with moldy cars either lacked discretionary funds or had higher priorities. The old Nissan had its own case of incipient rust as well. It would have been much worse if her father hadn't run it through the car wash every week for years. Eastern cars rusted from the bottom up because salt was spread on roads to melt winter snow. Pacific cars rusted all over from the salty ocean breezes. In any case, Maybelle absolutely loathed the clunker, but had no choice. She simply had to attend this meeting and her folks refused to go. Her entire grade in journalism class, and maybe her future career, depended on it.

"Hiya Maybelle, how's tricks?"

"DON, shame on you! I am not a hooker and that is sexist language!" she spat back without real vituperation. Vocabulary expansion and learning the original meanings of common phrases were recent lessons in her journalism course.

"Wha…" started Don.

"Nevermind," huffed Maybelle, "pop just wants the tank topped off."

"Why surely lass," Don agreed, "glad te be o' service."

Thank Gahd Don was so easygoing, Maybelle reflected. That was probably not the best opening for a conversation with someone you wanted to extract information from, she ended her thought with.

"So Don," she queried with maximal innocence, "hear any comments from your customers about the meeting tonight?"

"Looks like yer right rear tire might have a slow leak, Maybelle. Good idea te fix it soon. I could…"

She cut him off, "No time for that now, Don, I have to report on the meeting tonight for my journalism class!

Didn't anyone say anything?"

"Lots of small talk," Don replied. "Stan believes his vision will secrete a multitude of benefits for us all."

"Wow, Maybelle gushed, "can I quote you on that?"

"Lass, ye put de words in me very own mouth."

"Great!" she replied, oblivious to his irony. "Here, I made my own business cards."

Other than the occasional mushroom picker or an unfaithful Romeo, 6:30 on Tuesday evenings in mid-October was not usually a busy time. Don took a much-needed break to rebalance the hydraulic status of his body and then told the counter girl she could take off after she cleaned out the few remaining Jo Jo's and stale burritos from the warmer. Then he plopped his bum in the plastic lawn chair in front of the station's deli, lit up a cigarette, and speculated about the upcoming meeting. Annie would be stopping by soon, he would close up, and they would attend the show. He had been joking, though, about bringing his boxing gloves. His nose had already been broken too often in his youth. He anticipated spectator, not participatory, entertainment. Who knows, one of these development proposals might help his business too. It would be nice if Annie could leave behind the stress of supervising employees 8-5 and shift her time to the actual art work she enjoyed so much.

Funny, Don, mulled, he had not seen Grace or Johnny this evening. He had not even seen them drive by the station. Her light blue Toyota Prius was an unmistakable vehicle in this community. Maybe she didn't need a fill-up. Of all the participants that came to mind, they might have the best reasons to skedaddle promptly post-meeting.

∫

"Quiet! Quiet Please! We want to get started here. Quiet Please!" begged superintendent Bob Wilkins over the crackling old loudspeaker system as he simultaneously tried to speak through the handheld microphone and use both hands to wave the crowd to be seated. Few heard more than irritating noise, and those that understood mostly ignored him. Many heated conversations were already underway.

"ORDER please! Order!" Bob reverted to his style for addressing high school rowdies. "Let's all be seated so we can begin." Truth be told, the high school gymnasium was a horrid place to hold a public meeting, although Bob tried to take pride in the school's public service. The floor and walls of the gym reverberated every little sound and the lack of noise-dampening ceiling tiles didn't help. The tiles had been removed because kids who didn't make the basketball team found solace in busting them. The antiquated speaker system suffered from inadequate power, poor speakers, and bad connections. The seating consisted of folding metal chairs crammed too close together. The intent was to herd people close to the front in case the microphone failed. Many people chose the hard wooden audience bleachers to each side simply because they were less crowded. Others rearranged the chairs as needed. Sheriff Ray had had more than one reason to suggest the Lutheran church auditorium, but that was now beside the point. Maybe, if these proposed developments went through, there would be new tax revenues to build a decent community meeting hall. Or not.

It appeared that Bob was about to get more strident. Jeff Atkins approached the front of the stage and talked into his ear. Bob hesitated a second and then reluctantly handed off the microphone to Jeff. He had wanted to welcome folks to the high school for this weighty public meeting and officially introduce Jeff, but circumstances dictated otherwise. Jeff had more experience with such crowds and venues. He stood prominently up front and center stage. He held the microphone low by his side, looked at individual audience members that were eyeing him, and waited. Within two minutes the crowd was seated, fairly quiet, and focused on this government outsider.

"Good evening everyone," Jeff Atkins began, "for those of you who I have not yet had the pleasure to meet, I am the Community Input Coordinator for the Conservation Division of the State Department of Natural Resources." Even subdued murmurs sounded like a low rumble in this gym, but Jeff simply waited them out.

"As you all know, the state of Oregon values the opinions and input of its citizens." Snide comments bubbled up in response to that statement.

"Part of the process of approving new developments, especially those that impinge on natural resources in any way, involves public meetings so that everyone has their say and important issues are discussed." The audience groan sounded like a troll with indigestion. "The purpose of this meeting tonight is to discuss two development proposals that affect the same set of natural resources. The proposals are the Joint Cranberry Bog Expansion Project proposed by the Cranberry Farmers Association and the Lucky Dunes Casino Project proposed by the Confederated Tribes of the

Sand Coast."

The murmur rumble increased a little. It was still only about Richter 1.

"I will first give you my perspective on these projects, and then introduce the panelists seated before you on this stage." Hardly necessary, thought many audience members.

"I understand fully that both of these projects entail considerable potential benefit to the local economy. Put bluntly, that means many individuals here might profit." Murmur rumble: Maybe Jeff is human?

"I also know that some members of the community oppose one or both proposals, and that there are several other pertinent factors to consider." Murmur rumble: Maybe not.

"First, both proposed projects impinge significantly on very rare wildlife and plant habitats that occur almost nowhere else in the world. Like it or not, the state, the country, and the world is watching what is happening here." Murmur rumble: Is this guy threatening us?

"Also, I know for a personal fact, that neither the CFA nor the tribe have consensus among their members about the wisdom of proceeding." This comment resulted in significant stares among audience members and panelists seated on the stage.

"Both the state of Oregon and the relevant federal agencies have now tentatively approved each project individually, but the projects conflict to some degree and their cumulative impacts, if both were to be implemented, are not acceptable in terms of habitat loss. We have a quandary here folks." Murmur rumble: Well, Duh! At least Jeff knew the value of understatement.

"Before I introduce our panelists and open the discussion, I want to personally thank the representatives of both the CFA and the Confederated Tribes, as well as their lawyers. They all have been exceptionally patient in dealing with state and federal bureaucracies and our all-too-cumbersome application and approval process. They have been courteous and professional. They have carefully filled out and submitted all the requisite paper work. Most importantly, their arguments have been thoroughly researched and well-documented." Murmur rumble: Maybe he is human after all?

"Although all parties and their lawyers have been fully cooperative, neither of the proposals has yet to adequately address their joint jeopardy to the affected ecosystem." Murmur rumble (approaching Richter 2): Maybe not.

"The development proposals open for discussion tonight ... " Boisterous Bob Newall could constrain himself no longer. He bolted upright and shouted, "So when will we discuss them!?" Decorum, propriety, and rules of order also were not prevalent local skills. Enough people were interested in what Jeff was saying though, that Bob got no positive feedback and he sat down again. "... are ones that I have tried hard to ensure all the community understands. I have frequently discussed the issues with your local newspaper, and my department has sponsored local distribution of pamphlets and fliers. All the libraries along this portion of the coast have received the relevant public documents for anyone to view. I have made sure that local TV programs have covered the issue and a great deal of information has been posted on our web site for those of you who use computers at home or in your library." Murmur rumble: Who has time? (Gossiping was easier and more enjoyable).

"The individuals who sit on our panel tonight are important members of your community who have a stake in what is decided and who have agreed to represent these proposals or alternate viewpoints. I will very briefly introduce each, since most of you know them well anyway. They can speak for themselves. I will also be a member of the panel for questions concerning state regulations." Murmur rumble: Maybe not human, but at least he didn't drone on with government platitudes.

"First, on your left is Ole Gorseman. He is one of the south coast's most successful cranberry farmers and founding member of the CFA. His collaboration will be instrumental to the implementation of the JCBEP proposal because his farm includes essential irrigation rights. Next to him is Bugsy Sopp, current president of the CFA. Next is Wally Jackson, tribal head for the Confederated Tribes of the Sand Coast. Seated by him is Stanley Latterly, real estate developer for the tribe. Next is Mary Jackson, a tribal elder who opposes the casino plan in its current form. Unfortunately, two invited panel members are absent. Frank Horner from the Bureau of Land Management is not able to make it tonight. He has made it clear that the Department of Interior opposes both developments because their noise and activity would likely discourage the migrating Aleutian cackling geese from using the newly created National Wildlife Refuge they have dedicated nearby. He told me their position is on record, but that they felt they had little say in this matter because the refuge is not immediately adjacent to the affected lands." Snickering chuckles roamed the crowd this time.

"I am more disappointed to report that Grace Flores, the representative from The Conservancy, has not yet arrived."

"Yeah, where is she?" Stan replied loudly behind Jeff's back. "She's been bugging this community for nearly a year now about our projects and now she won't even show her face at the community meeting! Coward!"

Jeff was annoyed at being interrupted so rudely by a panelist, but he did not disagree with Stan's opinion. "So, now I am going to hand the mike back to Bob to referee the questions and conduct this meeting. Thank you all." Big mistake, reflected Sheriff Ray, who had discreetly positioned his deputies around the gymnasium. Maybelle stood uncomfortably close, but she was too focused on the stage and scribbling her notes to notice his deployment.

In terms of useful discussion or resolving issues, the meeting only devolved from there. In terms of a spectator sport, it improved immensely. Maybelle wished she had borrowed her dad's old cassette tape recorder. She couldn't keep up. White conversation noise approached Richter 3 and made hearing panelists very difficult, although the floor usually hushed enough to listen to audience members voice their opinions. Bob was wholly ineffectual and eventually just let things take their course.

Ole was typically soft-spoken and understated. He simply responded to pointed inquiries with vague statements that there might be a better way that would also preserve more of the natural bogs. Few knew what to think of his unexpected comments and some wondered if the night in question had affected his sanity.

Bugs defended the CFA's plans as best he could without Ole's full-fledged support of further development on their lands. It was a very awkward situation for him. Bonny (in the audience) felt his discomfort and wondered about Ole.

Wally said little in response to questions. This forum was so disorganized and disrespectful that he decided to just go through the motions. He reiterated the contributions and taxes his tribe promised to the local community in exchange for their approval. He personally felt that he should not have to remind them of this. The settlers had stolen their land, so why should the community, county, state or feds profit from returning sovereignty over a tiny piece of sandy land to the tribe? He didn't say that.

Stan declaimed as usual about the extraordinary and unending economic benefits that the casino would bring to the community. In keeping with his newly pronounced green credentials, he expounded on the sustainable construction and energy efficiency of the planned casino. He suggested that the JCBEP also should be allowed to proceed. Who needed the bogs anyway? Nobody profited from them. It was their bogland; they should be allowed to grow cranberries if they wanted. The audience grew bored and antsy as his predictable tirade dragged on. The attention of those who cared less started to drift. Some nodded off.

In the lull that ensued as Stan was winding down, Mary cleared her throat, stood up, walked around the panelist table and took center stage. Like Jeff, she looked individual audience members in the eyes and quieted the crowd. Most respected her and wanted to hear what she had to say, even if they disagreed.

Mary said, "My clan has lived on the land of the dunes and bogs since time immemorial. It has been our home and our sustenance for countless generations, but we never considered it 'our land.' How can a people own the creation from which they arise? Now the small piece of reservation land that our confederation of tribes holds in stewardship has lines drawn around it. People have started calling it 'tribal land.' These proposed developments, as they are now planned, will wash away forever the last vestiges of our heritage and traditions. We all live on the south coast now. How will we choose to live together? Do we choose McBurgers, McMansions, McCranberries, and McCasinos? Isn't there a better path? I see a way that provides us all with respectable livelihoods while maintaining our culture and enriching our souls. Do you not see it too? We need to act more thoughtfully, for the well-being of the land and all the peoples who dwell upon it."

The audience processed her words for a moment as they struggled to understand all she had implied. Then it erupted into a sea of discordant voices. Approaching Richter 4, Sheriff Ray calculated. He would intervene when the cacophony reached 5 and the building started to shake. Stan erupted from his seat and stomped toward Mary on the stage to confront her directly. Shouted comments like "What's wrong with McBurgers?" or "Go live in a bog if you want!" clashed with earnest entreaties that Mary had very good points that had not yet been properly considered. Mary ignored Stan's ranting and returned to her seat, composed and content with her voiced stance.

Holly Darlington, who had been sitting in the front row, got up and walked calmly onto stage. The commotion lowered to R2 as some in the audience strained to hear what she had to say. "Most of you know that my family settled here a hundred and fifty years ago, near the dune lands that are now slated for development. We were always poor. We were laborers. We felled the forest and dug out the tree roots. We drained the natural bogs and excavated the new rectangular cranberry bogs. To control flooding, we built berms around them. We dug irrigation ditches and diverted streams. The native peoples who had lived here for God knows how long had mostly been removed already. We picked cranberries side-by-side with the few who did remain, but my family did not own a farm. We homesteaded the pine forests on the higher dunes because no one else wanted that infertile land. But enough is enough! Now this community is talking about paving over or ripping up the few remaining natural bogs and dunes for economic development!" What's next? The ocean? The sky?" The rumble increased to R4 again and Sheriff Ray fidgeted.

Holly grabbed the heretofore-unused microphone and boomed, "Hear Me Out!" Down to R2 with a lot of latent resentment brewing.

"These are not the only developments proposed around here." No one could dispute that.

"What about the proposed 'world-class' golf course and resort on the north bank of the Switches? Do we want that special area reserved for only rich visitors? What about the huge chromite mine being proposed near Sandstone Point by the Global Minerals Corporation based in New

Caledonia? Do we want them to dig up 2 million year-old sand deposits to send a constant stream of noisy, polluting dump trucks tearing up our county roads? Do we want toxic metal pollution of our wells? Do we want to destroy the scenery and solitude that attracts tourists and their dollars by the thousands? What about the windmill and wave energy projects that are being proposed here? Where will they go and what will they affect? Most importantly, what will be the impact of allowing all of them at once? The hubbub will be deafening! All this talk about 'my land' is missing the point! We… "

The assembly's uproar had becoming deafening and Holly's voice was drowned out. The sheriff was about to intervene. Sally went on stage and dragged her mother off before she became the target of rotten vegetables. Stan was shouting something. Everyone in the audience seemed to be arguing with their neighbors or the stage. Bob cowered, completely flustered. Then punches were thrown in one tight knot near the bleachers and a few teenage troublemakers took that as their opportunity to stoke the brawl with pushing and obscene provocations.

Sheriff Ray climbed quickly onto the stage and shouted at the top of his considerable lungs and voice, ENOUGH! The command blended into the gym's reverberations and had little effect. People were being pushed and shoved. Innocent attendees were being endangered, especially women, children, and older people. Ray grabbed the microphone from Bob and tried again, but Stan had ripped the wire off the amp with his boot when he had stormed to the front of the stage to confront Mary. Ray looked at the distant thin gym ceiling and judged the risk to bystanders and the school's repair budget to be slight compared to the danger of letting this public brawl continue. He drew his Glock 9 mm pistol, aimed it upwards and back at an angle toward the hopefully vacant football field, and shot it once through the ceiling. Better than tasers, he figured.

Shocked silence descended on the assembly following the blast. Steeling himself to chastise his neighbors, the rear doors burst open and in strode dual forces of nature.

Chapter 8 — Peering Past

"At least two strong spirits inhabit the bog and the grove." Mary said. Grace gaped at her, more dumbfounded than Johnny. "I met them thirty-two years ago. Tonight we will again. Tonight all things turn for us, for you, for our tribe, for the land, for the bog and grove. Now is the time."

"Mamaw, you're creeping me out! This sounds like some kinda supernatural horror movie!"

"Peace, Grace. Our actions will be dangerous, but if things go as I foresee, the results will be transformative."

Johnny sat unperturbed, looking at Mary with curiosity and some guesses. Mary returned his gaze with a slight tweak of the corner of her lips that could be construed as a hint of a shared-secret smile, but which was hidden from Grace. Neither had shared the tale of his bog experience with her yet. Soon.

Grace became more insistent. "Dangerous? Transformative? Explain yourself, mamaw!"

"Chill, Gracie dear. Hear your mamaw out. Have you lost all your patience and open-mindedness?" That comment struck home, and deeply, exactly as Mary had intended. Grace prided herself in tolerance, however she was not always aware of what all that entailed. Now was a good time for her to relearn some of the manners traditionally practiced by her people.

"The three of us are going to go on a, well, what shall we call it? A joint vision quest!"

Johnny started to snicker at the unintentional play on words. Mary stopped him with her semi-feigned gaze of disapproval. Grace missed their silent communication again. She was trying to figure out what mamaw meant.

It seemed like her adoptive mom could always arrange a meeting without inviting anyone to it. Only a couple of weeks after she had moved back in for the duration of the bog project, mamaw had negotiated with Lillie next door to let Grace use her Wi-Fi network rather than going to the library each morning to check her email. Mamaw knew I would be here this morning, Grace thought. The bookstore and coffee shop were closed on Mondays and Tuesdays, so it was a perfect time for her to concentrate on emails and writing. It was certainly much nicer sitting quietly in the back nook (closest to Lillie's house), with Freda and a Moche mocha, than going to the depressingly antiseptic library to work. Johnny did chores for Mary now, but he usually didn't stop by when Mysty Pages was closed. Did she trick him into showing up today? Oh, I'm thinking like a paranoid conspiracy theorist, Grace admonished herself. Maybe mamaw simply asked him to stop by this morning.

"Mamaw," she pleaded, "I have work to do. I need to finish this bog reserve proposal in time for the big community meeting next week. Then I need to run it past some reviewers in the Conservancy before they commit to my ideas and plans."

"It can wait," Mary said definitively, "tonight you both will learn how your heritage pertains to this issue. It is the most important wisdom you can ever attain. I insist. Pack now. We will have a long walk. Bring water, warm clothes, and a blanket to sit on. We will be staying overnight."

Overnight?! Grace was about to object again, but after one look at Mary, deferred to her will as a tribal elder more than as a mother. She couldn't deny that getting out on the dunes again, especially with these two dear ones, would be effective therapy for her overworked soul. All the stakeholders that promoted or contested the two development plans seemed to be remarkably intransigent. How can I possibly get them to agree on anything, she thought, especially what I want? Some perspective and clarity might indeed be in order.

For that matter, what did mamaw mean, two strong spirits?

∫

The Datsun was now officially pursuing its second calling as a curb ornament and Johnny had no car, so Grace drove her Prius. It wasn't far, but the Prius was not good off-pavement, so they would be hoofing it some distance.

"Turn here," Mary directed. Grace hesitated.

"Doesn't the elderly Weatherby couple live in this dilapidated old house? Why are we turning down their driveway?" Grace asked, as she pulled in alongside the decaying, gothic style picket fence that bulged outwards towards them. The rickety barrier barely contained the overgrown yard of the long-unpainted, moss covered,

Queen Anne styled residence. The Weatherbys had not had a trick or treater in fifteen years.

"It isn't only their drive. It is also access to the south side of the reservation. Not many people know about this lane, but it's a tribal right of way. If you were driving Wally's rig, we could take it for another couple of miles, right down to the edge of the Wayward River. The lane is getting sandy though; perhaps you should park in that pullout there. It is unlikely that any tweekers will find or burglarize your car here. It should be safe. I know some paths that start around that next bend."

Grace and Johnny donned backpacks with their provisions. Mary pulled the strap of her woven carryall bag over her head onto the opposite shoulder and across her chest, then shifted the bag behind her. They started northward along the trail, and shortly Mary led them on a fork that headed west. Johnny had expected them to continue north to the bogs.

"Where are we going?" he asked.

"I'd like to show you a special area," Mary replied, "This was where the dunes tribe dwelt for countless generations."

"Are we on reservation land now?" Grace asked.

"Yes. The property line is just south of the lane where we parked. The reservation stretches from the sea to Highway 101 and north from this southern edge for various distances. Along the highway, we only own a 5 mile stretch before our land is bounded on the north by the Gorseman and Sopp cranberry farms. Closer to the sea, our land continues another 20 miles farther north until it is bounded by the BLM and the Aleutian Goose National Wildlife

Refuge."

"Last month," Grace replied, "when Twarn and I flubbed that field trip, we entered the swamp, bog, and forest part of the reservation at a spot that is partway down the road that runs along the south side of Ole Gorseman's farm. I've never been on this duney part of the reservation closer to the ocean before." Maybe Grace hadn't, but Johnny had. He still didn't mention his abortive vision quest. Not yet anyway.

It was a warm sunny fall day. After a pleasant stroll, they approached a small river with sandy banks.

"This is the Wayward River, I presume," Johnny noted.

"Yes," Mary answered, "it cuts a meandering path through our lands on its way to the sea. It always has, but it rarely slices the same path from year to year."

"I know," Grace added, "I have studied a lot of historical maps of this area for my bog preservation proposal, and the river never seems to be depicted in the same place twice."

They had rounded a bend in the erratic river. Just when Johnny was about to ask why, Mary said, "Look. Tell me what you think that is." She was pointing to a long object sticking out of the opposite bank. It might have been driftwood from a young tree, but it was white and curved smoothly. "It looks like a huge rib bone, but what…" Grace stopped short, amazed, "is that a whale bone?"

"Good guess, daughter. Indeed it is. Our tribe never hunted whales at sea, but every few years one would wash up on shore. When so gifted, our people feasted and then used the bones for ornamental and ceremonial purposes."

Johnny's excellent eyes were big with wonder as he scrambled as close as he could get to it on their side of the river. "It looks like the bone has been etched or carved!"

"Correct again," Mary replied. "Our lodges were built with cedar planks, but whalebones often adorned the entrances or created archways inside. They were usually carved with images depicting our traditions or with the characters in our origin and morality tales that we told around the lodge fires during the long wet winter months. We are now in the general area where the main village was usually located. Like the river, though, the exact location shifted. Steady summer winds off the sea would block the river with drifting sand and force it into a new course. Sometimes the river would gobble up lodges as it wandered, and sometimes the lodges had to be moved closer to where the river had shifted. Lodges and bones were buried and unburied as the dunes migrated. Even now, with all this beach grass stabilizing the dunes, the caretaker at the wildlife refuge up north checks the outlet to the Wayward River every day. If sand blocks the stream, it can flood nearby cranberry farmers when they don't want the water."

"Why did your dunes tribe build their lodges here?" Johnny puzzled aloud. "It seems so exposed and it must have been a hassle to move the lodges so often. Besides, what did they eat, sand?"

"They … " Mary started.

"Well … " began Grace. They looked at each other and laughed.

"You take the why, mamaw, and I'll fill Johnny in on what they were likely to eat here."

retorted, "Only if they were trying to get away from braves like you!"

"Seriously though, they only had to walk a few miles north or south to collect shellfish. They could spear and net all the salmon, steelhead, trout, and lamprey they wanted from the Wayward River. The bog-lands had plenty of waterfowl. Because the ponds and lakes here are small, it was easy to hide along the edge and hunt with arrows or nets. Berries were abundant in the fall, and where there are berries, there are bear to hunt."

"Berry ass-toot," commented Johnny as he dramatically navigated another steaming, black, black bear, berry turd.

Grace noted he was more observant and graceful than Wally had been last month, but she would not give Johnny the satisfaction of saying so after his recycling of the community pun in yet another awful version.

"They also used their atlatls and spears, or later, bows and arrows, to hunt the deer and elk that frequented the edges of the marshes." she continued. "They trapped beaver, muskrat, mink, martens, and otters for food, or for pelts, or both. Children were encouraged to catch or gather turtles, frogs, salamanders, newts, and eggs."

"Not precious plover embryos!" Johnny egged her on.

Johnny and Wally did seem to have inappropriate plover witticisms in common. "I think they were much more abundant then," she rolled her eyes, "anyway, there were many other bird eggs too. Cattail and skunk cabbage roots were winter staples. I can picture proud braves like you grubbing around for them in the swamps all winter long.

"Seriously though, our dunes tribe also traded with neighbors, such as your hills tribe, Johnny, for bulbs, roots, and seeds that grow in the valley, hills, or mountains. Of course the occasional sea mammal such as beached whales, sea lions, or seals speared from rocky outcrops added copious fat to the diet." Grace ended with an unsuccessful grab at Johnny's midriff.

All three of them halted, fell quiet, and watched in wonder more than fear. There, not more than 10 yards away, was a mother black bear with her two seven-month-old cubs. All three bears were looking at all three people. The bears each had purplish berry juice covering their black snouts. Bits of berry skins, green leaves, and twigs stuck out from between their teeth. The mother bear did not seem protective of her cubs. They were old enough to scrap for themselves. In fact, none of the bears showed any fear or inclination to depart. Were they drunk on fermented berries? Obviously, they did not intend to vacate this berry patch. In fact, mama bear went back to browsing and the cubs followed suit after their fleeting curiosity was satisfied. Mary, Grace, and Johnny just backed up a little ways, took another route, and circled around the blissful bears.

Grace sidled up to Johnny and gave him a sideways hug. They exchanged a meaningful look and then pulled Mary in for a brief group hug. They all knew a poignant experience when they shared one. Words were superfluous.

They walked on quietly now, savoring the declining daylight and the wildness around them. Continuing east, they started weaving their way through swampy lowland meadows with rushes and sedges. A great blue heron leisurely lifted with powerful wing thrusts from a nearby pond. A belted kingfisher flashed by on its way to a better fishing perch. When they passed the reeds of a larger swamp they heard a "kick, kick, kid-di-dick" sound and finally saw the almost perfectly camouflaged Virginia rail standing with its head and beak pointed straight up. They startled a couple of does that bounded off. Clouds had moved in as the day wore on; they held the sun's heat like a blanket so the evening was likely to be unseasonably warm. A gentle onshore breeze brought the scent of the sea. Pines and evergreen bushes grew on the higher hills of sand while the low-lying areas oozed moisture. The gnats and mosquitoes of spring and summer had mostly disappeared with the onset of autumn. Passageways between the pines, swales, and increasingly dense shrubs were carpeted with pale white reindeer lichens; their ghostly luminescence transfigured the lanes into glowing faerie footpaths. Mushrooms, edible and exotic, grew in great profusion on the floor of the deepening forest; some erumpent specimens mimicked the lichens with their ghostly hues.

It was becoming more difficult to see, but Mary seemed to know her way, and neither Grace nor Johnny was anxious. Several hundred yards farther on, they ran across some deeply carved dune buggy ruts in the sand. The parallel slashes headed at a slight angle off from the direction they had come. The trio had not seen many dune buggy tracks during the day. The major storm that blew through last week had obliterated most of the recent tracks with what Mypps called "dops" for down pours.

"What are these!?" Grace yowled. "I know that some dullards trespass on reservation lands to ride their obnoxious fossil fuel dinobuggies, but this is a major rutway! Wait. Is this the track I've seen on Google satellite images? I thought that was an access road."

"Just that," replied Mary calmly, "it is a right of way called a traditional use prescriptive easement."

"A what?" Grace bristled.

"Come on Grace," Mary countered, "you work for the Conservancy. You know what easements are."

"I thought those were to prevent development, not rip a path through the property." she pouted.

"Well," said Mary "prescriptive easements mean that if you have blatantly been doing something without permission on someone else's property for x number of years and the landowner doesn't stop you, then you have an assumed right to continue. This rut leads from the end of Ole's southern road and wraps around through reservation lands to connect up to one of the refuge roads up north. It has been used since settler times, although it was traversed with wagons and livestock back then. It came with the reservation deal. The tribe is still trying to figure out how to close it off. Meanwhile, Twarn does a good job of informing us who strays from the rutted track. He can recognize many different tire prints, and he is good at photographing the patterns and matching them to buggies he sees around the area. I suppose just picking mushrooms gets boring. Good thing he hasn't been lynched. Sheriff Ray has busted enough local trespassers that now only the out-of-towners get away with venturing off this path, and not very many of them know about this right of way in the first place."

Grace scrunched up her face in disgust.

Meanwhile, Johnny was becoming distracted by their

proximity, in time and space, to his and Grace's impending transformations.

Grace, on the other hand, had been subconsciously blocking specific references to "the bog" and "the grove" from her thoughts. Half-hopefully, she said, "Do we hike out along the roads now, Mary? I thought you said something about staying overnight and communing with spirits, but we are practically back to civilization."

"On no, Grace," Mary said mysteriously, "Now comes the interesting part. This rut might cut through it, and it is only a short hike out to Ole's south road, but you and I both know that this strip of natural bogs between the cranberry farms and the dunes is the most important part of the reservation. Not just in terms of its unique ecosystems, endangered species, and all that, but also historically, culturally and spiritually. This zone has been special to both the dunes and hills tribes for uncounted millennia. Our tales are focused here. Our ceremonies were conducted here. Our ancestors are buried here. Before settlers, this bog zone extended several more miles eastward to the foothills. Now most of it has been converted to ranches, cranberry bogs, and the development along Highway 101. Countless grave sites have been violated and lost. Sacred places are now farmed and paved. Only this thin sliver persists, on the edge of the shifting dunes. We treasure it."

Grace didn't know how to respond to that. She looked at Johnny. His eyes seemed particularly animated when he turned to her.

He said, "Ole's creepy bog and the strange oak grove are about a half-mile that way."

"I know," she replied, "we visited it on our field trip last month."

Johnny looked in that direction. "That is where I meet the spirits too. Where Ole and I saw the bog maiden. Where the gaggle freaked."

Grace's lower jaw slackened. She was speechless.

Before Grace could recover, Mary adjusted her sling bag and said, "Come. We have a meeting tonight." She plunged without further explanation into the darkest, densest part of the reservation's forested bog lands and headed for Ole's forbidding bog and grove. They hurried not to lose her.

∫

A full harvest moon shone behind the clouds. Occasionally its disk could be discerned as the clouds temporarily thinned, but mostly it illuminated the billowy puffs from behind. The threesome found their way effortlessly to the oak grove at the edge of Ole's haunted bog and entered it with deep respect and cautious footsteps. Sure enough, the strange *Amanita* mushrooms were still fruiting. Perhaps another fresh flush had sprouted since Grace's field trip because it had rained so hard again last week. The mushrooms and grove appeared almost like a black and white cartoon in the diffuse moonlight. Amanitas of all sizes and degrees of cap expansion lined up in three semicircular arcs. Two large arcs overlapped and one small one, consisting of older, more decayed mushrooms, was off to one side.

Mary chose a spot in the grove where they could sit

and face the two main mushroom arcs while also looking out past them to the bog beyond. The minor older arc was within sight to the left.

"Settle yourselves comfortably. We will be here overnight. Put on your warmer clothes, drink some water and attend to nature if you need to, so that you will not be distracted later. I plan to enter a trance to share with you the old tale of our tribes. This way of remembering and telling is a tradition that my lineage of mothers passed, one to another, down to me. My grandmamaw, when she was already old and crippled, took me to this very spot when I was a young woman. She showed me how to do this remembering. When I succeeded, I not only recalled our history, I also caught haunting and vivid glimpses of the spirits that still abide here. Their desperate need scared me witless. I have never returned until this day. Now is the necessary time. NOW, both of you need to know."

Grace was covered in goose bumps. Know what!?

Johnny listened intently. Neither spoke.

"Our history, our ritual traditions, our tribes, this bog, this grove, these spirits, and our destinies are all intertwined," Mary warned. Then she continued with cautious enthusiasm, "Tonight, however, we have the chance to dispel a dreadful ancient anguish, and in doing so, find new and better paths for ourselves and for our now confederated tribes. Dress yourselves in courage. Let your love for each other guide and protect you tonight!"

Grace and Johnny looked at each other and knew Mary saw their love truly. Even the dim moonlight was unnecessary for them to acknowledge that understanding to each other with their gazes.

"I will be emptying my mind before I speak. I will be looking back beyond words. When I do chant the rememberings, what I utter will be in simple phrases that are dense with meaning. Prepare your own minds to soak up this understanding. Let your identities slip away. Drop your worried thoughts."

"We don't have much practice at that mamaw," Grace noted timidly.

Mary nodded. She was more concerned for her daughter and Johnny than they would ever comprehend.

"I know. Just try. I read a lot in my bookstore, you know. Sometimes words can actually be a tool to still the mind if they are repeated to exclude anxious thoughts or if they create an image of calmness. One verse that sticks in my mind is by an obscure oriental poet who once wrote:

Quieting the mind
deep in the forest
water drips down.

"Imagine water dripping in a forest until your mental ramblings get bored with themselves."

Grace liked that image. She and Johnny settled themselves as Mary also prepared herself. Then Mary started humming, eyes closed, rocking slowly forward and back, intoning the subtly complex melodies of her birthright.

Grace and Johnny found it surprisingly easy to concentrate on Mary's ritual crooning and discard their worldly concerns. Grace let go of her anthropological perspectives and bog preservation goals. Johnny tossed aside notions of who he was, should be, or might be.

Time passed. They focused on Mary's rhythmic vocalizations, their shared trance, the endlessly emergent moment. They opened themselves to ancient neglected memories: from the land, from their ancestors, from watchful spirits. These primal memories flowed through their awareness like a deep and languid river of memory. At some point, Mary's chanting had taken the form of words and phrases that floated like concept-leaves scattered along the still surface. Later, remembered words or phrases would simply be hooks to evoke the full depths of the experience, like a dream image or smell can unleash a flow of feelings, impressions, and recollections.

> We are the people of the water's edge
>
> The Trodders of the Far Mist
>
> With our deathless shaman
>
>
> We live on the edge of the sunrise water, with pines and seals
>
> We live on the edge of the midday water, with snow and game like houses
>
> We live on the edge of the sunset water, with pines, and bogberries
>
> We come from the big water
>
> On the water's edge we wander
>
> The Far Wanderers
>
> With the shaman who does not die

Now we live on the sunset water

On the dunes

By the bogs

We live here more years

Than the count of ten relatives

In ten families

In ten villages

In ten tribes

We learn new Nows in the land of dunes and bogs

New Nows, here by the sunset water

The shaman takes our memories and he walks into
a bog

The shaman beyond death, he walked into a bog
and lost his life

Cursed beyond death, the shaman bound the bog to
our fate

Cursed beyond death, the shaman bound other
spirits too

Now the bog protects us, the people without a
shaman

Now the bog spirits protect us, the people without
a shaman

They protect us, with their unbroken curse

The land burns, the hill tribes burn the land

New green trees stand up from the roots of black trees

The bog does not burn; it is too wet

The sand does not burn; it is too dry

Winter storms howl with fury from beyond time

Mountains of sand roam

Tall trees lie down and rivers lose their way

The people of the dunes are not harmed

The bog does not fill with sand

Some years, the sky does not weep

The land becomes brown

The small streams go away

The people pick up the fish

The bog stays green and wet

The people drink.

Rumbles from afar spook the game

The skies turn brown, then black

Grey sand falls from the sky like warm snow

Mud falls from the sky like dirty rain

The land is dark and cold

The people eat whale blubber and dry berries

Next year, the land is very green

The bog has more mosquitoes.

A ball of fire runs across the night sky

The sunset water eats it

The people fall down on the ground and cover their ears

Tall waters eat the sand

Hot fog blows over the land and the rain burns skin and leaves

The sun does not shine for a moon

The people hide in their lodges

The world does not end

The bog plants grow new leaves

The land shakes and the people are thrown down

Houses are thrown down

The tall water comes after the land shakes

The people go where the land sticks out, where the trees stick out

Some people tie their canoes to the trees

Sometimes the tall waters take away the lodges

Not the people, not the bog.

The people eat and dance in the sun again

The people go to the cursed bog on the day of high summer

The people have a big feast on the day of high summer

The people thank the Great Mystery for their Nows

There on the edge of the bog

The people leave before dusk

The people bury their ancestors near the bog

The bog protects them

The bog spirits protect them

The people fear the bog

The people fear the spirits of the bog

It is a lonely place

Strange rot-fleshes grow there

Strange ground-fleshes grow there

The river of memory slowed. The words floated downstream, away to the sunset water.

Mary, Grace and Johnny opened their eyes. Deep night had descended. Thick clouds now hid the moon; the remnant illumination was barely sufficient to see. The night remained warm and humid. Dense fog had gathered over the bog; tendrils of its vapor stretched into the grove where they sat. The branches of the grove seemed to reach toward them, inviting embrace. Each second dripped with latent anticipation, deep in the forest, quieting their minds, heightening their senses.

Mary spoke, quietly and reverently, "The bog spirit defends the tribe, the land, and the bog. The grove spirit, in turn, sustains her. He loves her and she him.

Now there is another threat. The same threat that drove the Far Wanderers from the sunrise waters. No spirits can defend this place from the greed of men. Our ancestral spirits have suffered long. Tonight you can release them. Tonight we join forces to defend the bog. Only the incarnate can oppose the greedy."

Mary's words sank in very slowly.

As they did, Mary got up and went to the mushroom arc nearest the bog. She picked a young mushroom. She then plucked another from the arc that stretched into the grove. Last, she went to the small arc of old decaying mushrooms off to the side. There she picked a big old mushroom and returned to sit by Grace and Johnny.

Mary gave Grace the mushroom she had picked from next to the bog; then she handed Johnny the one from within the grove.

"Here," she said, "eat." Then she started chomping down on the overly mature mushroom from the old arc. "I will ward off the malign spirit."

Grace felt like she was surfacing from a trance, struggling up through a vat of memory glue. She was about to grab mamaw's hand to stop her from consuming the rotten fungus. A verbal protest was forming on her lips when she half-swooned, her mind swirled, and her perceptions realigned. She shook her head to try to clear her vision. Betwixt moments, her consciousness snapped into crystalline lucidity. Others were here. This was the most important moment of her life, the most important moment of all their lives.

Unlike Johnny, Grace had never consumed mind-bending recreational drugs in her entire life. She had no experience with altered states of mind other than coffee, a few beers, or drowsiness. She looked at him imploringly, feeling deep trepidation. He had been watching her intently. He smiled his reassurance and nodded toward the mushroom she was holding. Then he took a bite of the mushroom Mary had given him.

Mary had already eaten most of her slimy toadstool. Johnny continued to eat his. Grace loathed mushrooms. They made her want to retch with revulsion. Still, if she couldn't trust her mamaw and the man she loved, whom could she trust? Perhaps that maiden hovering in the fog over the bog?

Chapter 9 — Tryst and Curse

I t seemed like she had been waiting her whole life; little did she know what waiting would mean. She had turned aside the amorous advances of every eligible young man in her tribe. Who now would mate with a maiden who would soon see her eighteenth summer? Unlike most tribes, the Far Wanderers had not interbred much with others during their long migration. They had come to believe, under their shaman's tutelage, that their lineage was pure. Mating with other peoples would only dilute their blood and traditions. They harbored no ill will toward others; they simply wanted to be left alone. They expected their young to marry and procreate within the tribe. She had felt no such compunction and had other reasons for wanting to mate. That is why she had experienced the tribe's consternation and suffered its ridicule. That is why they had given her the disparaging name of Waits for Love. She would know her man when she saw him, of that she had been certain. Then, he had held her in his arms even before she saw him.

"Stop sulking, Waits!" scolded her lodge mother, Tule Reed. "Our cook pots are nearly empty and it is not raining right now. We should gather more bulbs to fill the men's

bellies. Do they want to go out in the cold and hunt for
fresh meat? NOooo, they want to recline on their furs,
poke the lodge fire embers, smoke their kinnikinnick, and
tell beaten-to-death stories. We will go out and dig in the
swamps and marshes until our toes are numb, just like the
cold muddy roots we gather to feed our men. Come. Stop
brooding about love. Remember this day of grubbing for
roots for men when you think about their love."

Waits dejectedly muttered, "Yes matron." She slipped
a cushioning layer of moss into her oldest moccasins and
bound them as tightly as she dared. She threw short warm
furs over her shoulders and used a cord to cinch them
around her waist, but no lower. Then she grabbed the
basket that floated best, and followed her crabby lodge
matriarch to do her duties among the sodden reeds.

As she grubbed for roots, Waits for Love's mind
naturally wandered to her rescuer, the man for whom she
truly longed. His eyes were brighter than the flames he
stoked. His arms were warmer than a circle of suns. His lips
burned with passion for her. Stop it, she rebuked herself. It
did no good. Rooting in the swamp was worse than these
ridiculous mind games.

Plop.

Waits looked around, but saw nothing unusual. It was
probably just a bird pooping in the water. Strange though,
she had seen no bird.

She had only begun her mind games again,
when...plop.

It was quieter that time, but closer. She looked in the
direction where she had heard it. The shape of a young man
emerged part way from the nearby bushes and gestured

towards her. Her heart raced. Was it really him?

"WAITS! Come! I found many roots together over here. Help me gather them and we can get out of this cold smelly morass sooner. I cannot feel my toes."

Waits couldn't feel her toes either, but did not even think about that. He was here! Watching her! Plopping her! How could she possibly get away from her lodge mother? What would Love Flames think of a muddy maiden? Well, he had held a boggy maiden before. Maybe he would warm her up again!

Tule Reed was bent over, prying out roots. Waits stood bolt upright, looked straight at Love Flames hidden in the bushes. She raised her hand, signaling, "Wait." Then she hurried to help her lodge mother harvest as many roots as possible, as quickly as possible. There were no more plops. They soon left the swamp. Waits for Love glanced back. He cautiously showed himself again from among the bushes. She nodded, and signaled demurely, "Wait." "Soon."

They had returned only a little way towards the village.

"Lodge mother, you go ahead. I will wash these roots in the river before I bring them back to the men."

Old Tule Reed had poor circulation in her feet, so she gladly let Waits do the final task. After several further admonitions about thorough cleaning and haste, she hurried back to warm her toes by the lodge fire as she prepared to cook for the idle men.

Then he was there. His arms were warmer than a hundred lodge fires. His lips burned like hot embers of desire.

∫

No man had ever given Waits for Love flowers before. What a strange notion, collecting different flowers into a bundle. Flowers were everywhere, all around, but this marvelous man collected bundles of them to give her as a gift! It was silly really. Did he mean she was as pretty as the flowers, that the flowers made her prettier, or that she made the flowers prettier? Such riddles were only a distraction; his flower-bundle offerings warmed her heart as no words could.

Each bundle included different kinds of flowers as the spring grew toward summer. Sometimes he would mix in green leaves, grasses, twigs, tree beards, or even colorful ground-fleshes and tree hair. The mix of colors and textures were eye-catching. Each bundle was delightful in its newness. Each had a mixture of wonderful smells. He acted like he was giving her the earth, and with it, himself. Waits glowed with love; she no longer felt she was waiting, at least not for love. Mating was going to be another matter. They both knew it.

"Will you meet me tomorrow at the bog?" Love Flames pleaded.

"I want to Love, I truly do," she replied with disappointment, "but the whole tribe is going south along the beach this week to bring in the great whale that came to our shore. This gift gives us rich food for many moons, but everyone must help to butcher the noble creature, render the blubber, smoke the meat, and gather the bones. I must help!"

"Then let me come with you," Love pleaded. "I will help your tribe and prove my worthiness to be your mate."

Waits put her hands on Love's chest and looked up

into his fervent eyes. "No," she said softly, with regret. "It cannot be. Eagle Claws found the big water beast. He claims first rights after Chief Mountain Whale gets his ritual share. Eagle Claws has wanted me to be his mate since we were little children building sand lodges on the beach. He is always angry that I did not accept him. He waited so long for me to change my mind that all the other fine maidens were chosen and he had to mate with Willow Hair, the lowest maiden in my lodge. He treats Willow Hair badly and scorns me for rejecting him, but his large share of the whale will come to our lodge because he is mated to Willow Hair. If you come to help butcher the beast that he found, then he will loathe you even more. He might challenge you to a fight or he could give his whale meat to others, just to snub me. Our lodge needs his share. He is a strong provider. I cannot risk our lodge not getting Eagle Claws' meat, blubber and oil."

Love had only really heard the part about fighting Eagle Claws. "I am not afraid of this man who wants you. I will fight him and take his meat!"

"NO! No," Waits beseeched Love. "That must not happen. Not if we are to be mated. My tribe must agree. They do not forbid outside mating, but they judge such mates sternly. They must be convinced that your blood is as good as ours. We must show them all that you are a man of honor, not of quick or thoughtless violence. Later you should come to my lodge and make yourself better known, but not now."

Love reluctantly nodded his understanding.

"When I return," she continued, "we can visit your village together. I want to meet your mother and father, your lodge, your people. I will bring whale oil as a gift."

"My people do not need to meet you before we mate. I am expected to choose a woman from outside our tribe. I know they will be very pleased with you. But you can put some of that whale oil on your skin for me if you want…" Love flirted as he grabbed for her and they tussled playfully in the ferns.

♪

"Let's walk past the bog lake on the way back to your village," Love suggested, "I want to tell you about something that happened there last winter." He said no more.

"Why not?" Waits agreed, "I love the spot we first met. Now it is so green and full of new growth after the fire you lit sent me scrambling into the bog with breathing reeds." Her taunting words were a comfortable little joke between them now.

Waits asked no more about what he meant. He would tell her when the time was right. She felt like she was drifting in a canoe cloud through the sky. His family was incredible! They certainly liked the skin full of whale oil she had brought as a gift, but it had not been necessary to win their hearts. They treated her like a daughter as soon as they saw her. They laughed, feasted, and traded stories late into the night. His lodge was full of smiles. His tribe was large and peaceful. No one seemed to tell anyone else what to do. Each person seemed to come and go as he or she pleased; yet, they all gladly did what needed to be done.

Waits had never been to the inland hills before either.

There were so many new things to see, hear, smell and do. The camp dogs, the babies frolicking in the dust, the cone shaped lodges, the endless hills of brown grasses, gray-green mountains in the distance, and all the meat, skins, seeds and berries drying so nicely in the hot summer sun! Even the stream water seemed warmer and you could jump in from big rocks along the bank. She had never enjoyed swimming so much as when she and Love snuck off to his favorite pool. At least until little children eyes started peaking out of the bushes and Love was unable to shoo them all off at once! She still laughed to remember their squeals of delight at the pretend chase.

On their way back to her village, as they approached the small bog-lined lake where they had met, Love led Waits to one side of the strange little grove of oak trees. These were the first such trees Waits had ever seen. Love knew all about oak trees and she had seen many more during her visit just now to his village in the hills, but they both still thought these particular oaks were very unusual in their small stature and clumped form.

"I was hiding among the shrubs over here," Love said, "when I heard what your shaman said to your brother in this oak grove."

"What!?" This was one of Love's habits that really did frustrate Waits. He used so few words to say so much! Often, too, his remarks were like a grouse that bolted loudly into flight just at your side without warning. You could land on your butt from surprise.

"What do you mean, my shaman and my brother? What were they doing here together with you?" She stabbed him with her gaze. He had better explain this one fast.

Love looked properly stricken. She felt embarrassed by her strong reaction, but needed to know. Waits put her fists on her hips and waited. Responding like a big-eyed innocent seal, he said, "I was not 'with' them, I was already here. I was sitting quietly by the lake thinking about how to win your heart."

Waits' heart melted halfway, but she did not show it. He must still explain himself. Why had he not told her this before?

Love continued, "It was in the early morning, one day several moons after the new sun began to grow. I was here because only this place could sooth my ache to hold you again."

A little more melting, but not yet enough, she decided.

"Then I noticed a canoe paddle to a stop on the nearby river bank, followed by some shuffling. In the growing light, I saw your old, old, medicine man struggle to carry a young sleeping child. He was not able to carry the boy far, so he put him down, and then he stumbled to the edge of the oak grove to rest. The boy slowly awakened, got up, saw the shaman, and walked over to him. I could see then that he was your young brother, Wave Eyes.

"Why didn't you do something!?" Waits cut in.

"What?" Love responded, "There was no harm I could see. The old creature gave your nephew food and drink. He told the boy to listen. I decided to listen too. I remained very quiet and they never knew I was near."

Waits' heart was mostly thawed now as her curiosity overtook her frustration at not being informed earlier. She asked, "What did the bogman say?"

"Bogman? Why do you call him that?" Love's puzzlement was real. He had never heard that name for the shaman.

"His name is Beyond Old Gull," Waits replied, "We shorten it to Bog. It seems to fit because he led our tribe to these duney wetlands and does not want to leave. Now it seems he is sneaking around in bogs too! With my toddling brother, no less! What did he say?"

Love searched his memories and composed his thoughts. "The 'bogman,' as you call him, talked for a long time. It was almost midday when he finished. At first, I understood very little of what he said. He spoke in words I did not know. Later, I understood a little more as the words sank into my mind and became more familiar. I can only tell you the wide meaning, not the many little pieces. I felt like he was telling Wave Eyes about many, many lives, almost like they were all his own. Just as finding an acorn in a mussel shell makes no sense, his words did not match each other. Later, he started using more words from the tongue your tribe now speaks. Then I listened very closely, but still his words did not walk together in meaning." Love hesitated, then… "Please. Sit down with me, Waits. This will be very strange for you. For us. Let us sit together in this odd grove, by our boggy lake, and think about the meaning."

The day was warm and full. They had plenty of time to return the rest of the way home to her lodge today. Shafts of sunlight pierced the surrounding ancient trees and dragonflies flashed through these sharp beams for brief moments in their amorous flight. The world was suffused with lushness, fertility, and nowness.

Love put his arm over Waits' shoulder, pulled her close, and continued. "Your shaman, your bogman, talked of living forever. He talked about rot-fleshes and ground-fleshes. He talked about 'stretching' his life. He talked about 'jumping.' I think he meant jumping into a new life. He said that he was the tribe and always had been. He said that he and Wave Eyes would 'be one'."

"What?!" Waits exclaimed again as she jerked to the side so she could look at Love directly.

"That is what I think he said. That he and Wave Eyes would live 'together' forever. I do not know what that means. I did hear the bog shaman talk about coming back here when the late summer rains return. He talked about eating the yellow-spotted, red-capped ground-fleshes that grow in this grove. He sounded like he had been waiting his whole lifetime for this. I think he meant that the ground-fleshes that grew here would somehow let him and Wave Eyes come together and live on and on."

Waits for Love struggled to understand. Her many mind games about being with Love had never embraced such ideas. Living forever? Was the bogman going to force Wave Eyes to eat the ground-fleshes too? Why? Then another idea bubbled up. If two people could live forever, could they love forever too? Her heart sang with the possibilities. She knew instinctively that such thoughts were dangerous, treacherous, and maybe even deadly. She did not speak them. She shivered in the warmth of the day even with Love's arm over her shoulder.

∫

"Wave Eyes! Come to me! Here, let me hold you!"
Her family did not know what to think. Waits rarely
showed such affection for her boy brother. She hugged him
and stared around the lodge. The bogman was not there,
but Eagle Claws was. Love Flames had followed Waits for
Love into her lodge slowly and cautiously. He did not yet
feel welcomed by anyone in her tribe, nor in her lodge,
certainly not by Eagle Claws. Waits had insisted he come.
Her people had to get to know him if they were ever to
allow them to mate.

All fifteen members of her lodge stared at Love
Flames. The only one to speak was Eagle Claws.

"What is he doing here?"

The lodge patriarch, Thunder Sands, had no thunder
left in him. He was old, feeble, fat, near-sighted, and losing
his memories. He was once a fine man and good provider,
so the lodge cared for him. Now he had little say in lodge
decisions. Eagle Claws was the lodge's best hunter and
main provider of game. His will effectively ruled the lodge
and Waits suffered for it. After the warm welcome Love's
family and tribe had given her, she was both saddened and
emboldened by this cold reception.

Waits stated, "We have chosen each other, Eagle
Claws. You and all the tribe must accept this. Love is here
to learn our ways and to prove his worth."

"Worth?" Eagle Claws interjected, "Ha! What worth is
there in a man called 'Love?' Has he hunted anything bigger
than a slug? Does he know how to make good children
with his own slug? Will he spend his days poking the
embers of our lodge fire rather than you?"

Eagle's words were calculated to light fires of

resentment in Love Flames' heart. They succeeded. The last question was especially rude. Love started forward, but Waits put out her arm to stop him. She too was incensed, but waited a moment to choose her words carefully. Before she could continue, Eagle swaggered over to face Love Flames, inches away, brushing Waits aside. The men were of similar stature and build. Reciprocal hatred lanced from their eyes as they scrutinized each other's courage.

Eagle's move was almost too quick to see, but not for Love. Eagle Claws plunged his knife upwards toward the soft flesh just below Love's ribs. Love twisted away from the stab and grabbed Eagle's forearm in two places, with both hands. Love used Eagle's momentum to spin him sideways as he brought Eagle's arm down hard onto his rapidly lifted knee. Everyone in the lodge heard bones break. Eagle grimaced and twisted in an attempt to grab Love with his good arm. Love quickly lowered his leg and stuck his foot between Eagle's ankles, tripping him. Eagle landed hard on the side with his broken arm. He finally screamed his pain as the ends of the fractured forearm bones poked through flesh and ground in the dirt of the lodge floor. Eagle's rage momentarily overtook his pain as he struggled to regain his feet. Love kicked him in the face and Eagle fell back. His head cracked against one of the stones around the lodge fire, knocking him unconscious. The end of Eagle's braid landed in the embers and started to burn. The fight had taken but moments, but the whole of their world had changed, and not for the better, for anyone.

No one moved or spoke for a moment; such was their shock. Then Thunder Sands quavered, "Tule, come help me stand." Tule obeyed, helping the lodge patriarch to his unsteady feet. Thunder shambled slowly around the campfire and snuffed out the flame in Eagle's braid with his callused foot. He bent to get a closer look at Eagle's arm with his failing vision, then he straightened as best he could and peered at Love and Waits. "Eagle will lose his hunting arm, if he lives. You have taken food from the mouths of our lodge." Waits cowered, hugging her man, but Love stood upright, looked directly at Thunder, and said simply, "He tried to kill me. All saw."

"I did not see." Thunder replied. He turned to Willow Hair. "Go fast. Bring the bogman. We need a healer if your mate is to live." Willow choked back her sob as she raced from the lodge. Eagle Claws might mistreat her, but not always, and not in bed when he could pretend that she was someone else. His first son was in her belly. How would they feed their child now? Who would provide meat for their lodge? Curse Waits and her Love!

Love Flames knew it was senseless to flee. Running would be an admission of guilt. He had not started the fight. He put his arm around Waits; they backed up into a corner of the lodge near the door and waited. Thunder instructed Wave Eyes to lean with a stiff elbow and heal-of-hand on the inside of Eagle's upper arm to slow the flow of blood. Although young, he was hefty enough to staunch the bleeding. This skill was an important lesson for hunters and fighters. The lad could start learning now. He would also deal with the indirect consequences of his sister's actions. Responsibility came around. Waits cringed but did not object.

Soon, Willow crashed back into the lodge, struggling

for breath. "He is coming but he is OLD! He moves so slowly. I could not hasten him," she blurted between gasps.

"Build up the fire. Boil water," was all that Thunder said in response. Willow quickly bent to her tasks. Others shifted Eagle onto a clean fur.

After what seemed like ages, Beyond Old Gull entered. He showed no urgency, but he moved deliberately. He set aside several bags containing his healing medicines and tools; next he examined Eagle. He praised Wave Eyes for staunching the flow of blood and then corrected his form and encouraged him to continue. The shaman hardly glanced at the arm, but he saw blood on Eagle's hair so he examined his head where it had struck the rock. Then he opened each of Eagle's eyelids and examined his pupils. Nodding to himself with what seemed like some satisfaction, Long Gull stood and faced the offending couple. "What happened?"

Love Flames took a step forward. "He tried to kill me with a knife stroke under my ribs. I defended myself."

"A harsh defense," Long Gull noted wryly, "Why did you not just kill him?"

Love Flames did not waver. "I had no wish to kill. He acted in rage and I disarmed his rage."

Long Gull replied, "'Disarmed' is right. Bones in dirt causes festering that kills. He must lose his arm to save his life. You will answer for your deeds. Mountain Whale is being informed as I speak."

Long Gull looked at everyone in the Lodge, one by one. He felt more sadness than anything. "Thunder Sands, Tule Reed, Wave Eyes, you stay to help me. Flame-man and Waits, you also stay to watch what your choices have brought to this lodge and our tribe. All of the rest of you, leave now, I must cut off Eagle's arm."

Long Gull noted that Eagle had begun to stir. "You will hear screams. Be gone!"

All of the rest of the lodge members started to obey their shaman and healer, but Mountain Whale entered at that moment, blocking their exit. When he had squeezed in through their doorway, they quickly departed, Willow choking in dismay as she fled the impending amputation. The chief mountain settled his bulk onto an earthen ramp within the lodge. Guilt, judgment, punishment, and restoring balance would come later. Mountain Whale ignored Love Flames and Waits for Love. He had come to watch the healer work. He might be called upon to pin a squirming patient with his weight.

∫

The Dunes tribe was judging Love Flames for a second time. This time, what happened had been witnessed, the damage was done, and the tribe was overtly hostile. Eagle Claws would live, but without his favored hunting arm. He could learn to throw a spear with his other hand and arm, but never draw a bow again. The lodge would have to be supported in part by the tribe, and bitterness was inevitable.

Mountain Whale looked out over the crowded tribal lodge from his platform. He noted the angry faces, the heated conversations, the thrusting hand signals, the tension. It was his role to restore balance.

Mountain Whale lifted his hand and the lodge quickly

became still. He looked at Love Flames and Waits for Love and commanded, "Stand." They did.

"Unwanted man, you have taken the spear arm of one of our best hunters! Women will go hungry, babies will cry. The lodge of Thunder Sands will weaken, our tribe will suffer!" the mountain chief spat his accusations at Love Flames.

Love cringed at the hatred around him, but stood tall, and again, simply said, "Eagle Claws tried to kill me. I defended myself."

Almost before his words were out, the tribe roared their displeasure. Mountain Whale rose to his feet silencing them. His face was dark red with anger. "The lodge did not ask you to come! The tribe did not ask you to return! You could have left when Eagle confronted you. Instead you looked him in the eye and invited the attack!"

Mountain Whale and Love Flames were now throwing eye blades at each other like Eagle and Love had done right before the fight. Waits stepped boldly into the middle of the clash of wills and proclaimed, "I asked him to my lodge. I want him to become one with us. I want him to share our Nows. I want to be his mate!"

Her love had blinded her to her own tribe, to their traditions and beliefs. Even if she had tried, her words could not have been more inappropriate or more harmful to her and Love. The tribe burst into an uproar of disbelief, loathing, and malevolence. Mountain Whale, stunned by her selfish thoughtlessness, sat down and waited out the commotion.

Several young hunters, friends of Eagle Claws, brandished their weapons and loudly claimed the right to kill this outsider in combat and then tame the rebellious maiden with demonstrations of TRIBAL LOVE. An old woman shouted that the couple should be burned together in a large fire and many roared their approval. Several young children started flinging feces at the couple, but were dissuaded when their poor aim resulted in globs veering too close to the mountain. Mountain Whale let the menacing invectives continue long enough for the tribe to vent some anger, and for Love and Waits to fully understand their peril and the potential consequences of their misdeeds. This time he silenced the lodge with his booming voice. "NOW!"

The time of judgment approached. The chief had spoken the word of command. He wanted one more voice to be heard before he pronounced his judgment. "Beyond Old Gull," Mountain addressed Long Gull formally, "You are still our shaman, although many dislike you and your choices. You are our healer. You saved the life of Eagle Claws, although it cost his arm. You often talk of long visions and hidden considerations. Shorten and focus your sight now. Speak your thoughts on this matter quickly. Then I decide."

Long Gull had so far sat quietly at Mountain Whale's side during the tribunal. He looked at the tribe now. His tribe. His feelings were mixed. His people had become bickering animals. Maybe blood purity was not such a good idea in the long time or when circumstances changed? Maybe the tribe needed new blood to regain their dignity and vigor? These were all matters he would soon address. Once he had jumped again, he would have renewed vigor to undertake the task of reforming his people. He did not care about Love Flames. There were many nearby tribes with healthy young hunters. Bringing such fresh blood into the body and culture of the tribe would be hard, but he would have time. He did, however, care about Waits. She showed some of the passion and boldness that he felt more of the tribe should share. As he prepared to talk, he wondered, not for the first time, where his old bones were leading him.

"We have good relations with the tribes who dwell among the inland hills. We trade fairly with them, to our mutual wellbeing. They favor us when they burn the berry boglands. Even the bears are happy. Love Flames did not seek our maidens when he burned the bogs. He did not know she was there. He saved Waits from the cold water after she saved herself from the fire." A low grumbling arose among the tribe, but Long Gull waited them out. All knew that Mountain Whale would decide nothing until he had finished.

"Waits for Love, however, has never honored our mating traditions," he continued with a counterpoint. Many murmured their agreement. "She did not have the right to court Love Flames without her lodge's permission. Both Thunder Sands and Eagle Claws should have given their permission before she brought a man of another tribe to their lodge as a possible mate. She would have been even wiser if she had made her intentions known among the entire tribe. What she calls 'love' has blinded her to her place among us." More muttered their accord.

"Love Flames did not ask for violence. He defended himself. Eagle Claws harbored resentment born of Waits for Love's ill-considered and often repeated rejection of him as a mate. However, our traditions gave Eagle Claws a dubious reason for his resentment; we let him believe he deserved Waits simply because he was one of the tribe. Maybe before judgment is placed on these two, we should examine what we demand of our young when they choose a mate."

The Dunes Tribe was appalled. Not for the first time, Long Gull had contradicted his own teachings and questioned their fundamental beliefs. If it takes this long to gain wisdom, he pondered, how does any other tribe get by with only mortal wise-elders or healers?

That was enough bogman gull shit, Mountain decided, and roused himself. He glanced briefly at the sad old shaman who talked all around the decisions that must be made. Grasping his wisdom was like trying to grab foam skittering across a beach. Whale sat upright, as best he could. He looked over the gathered tribe and pronounced, "This is my decision!"

"Bring in Eagle Claws!"

Unexpectedly, several men immediately carried Eagle Claws in, slung on a long soft fur between two poles. It had only been one day since the bogman had cut off his arm just below the elbow and then burned the stump with fire to stop the bleeding and prevent the festering. He appeared somewhat delirious as his helpers propped him up on more furs in the middle of the lodge.

Mountain Whale proclaimed, "Waits for Love, you would have denied Eagle Claws your womb for his child, for a child of the tribe. Your choices resulted in this harm to him, your lodge, and our tribe. Now, I rename him Eagle Claw, and I give him the right to burn your womb with a brand from this tribal lodge fire.

"Love Flames, you claimed Waits for Love, but you are not of our tribe. You may stop Eagle Claw from burning her womb, but only by holding your hunting hand in front of her womb to defend it. Eagle Claw may burn your hand as much as he wishes as he stabs at her. Choose otherwise, and the tribe will burn you and Waits to death on the beach for all to witness."

Even Long Gull gasped at Mountain Whale's scheme for justice.

All complied. Waits for Love was uncouthly forced to sit open-legged before the stricken Eagle Claw. Love Flames crouched beside her. Eagle Claw grabbed a glowing brand from the fire and stabbed at Waits for Love's womb. Love Flames interposed his hand and held it there as the brand burned deeply into his palm. Eagle Claw shoved harder, but Love Flames gripped the brand with his fingers too, and held it. Eagle Claw lost his strength and resolve before he could plunge it further. Love Flames retracted the brand from his bubbling hand. Waits fainted. The smell of burnt flesh filled the lodge.

Mountain Whale stood again. "You will leave our village and never return Love Flames. We will kill you if you do. Waits for Love will now be mate to Eagle Claw; she will bear his children and she will work as two mates for feeding and helping her lodge. This judgment is complete."

Most agreed balance had been restored, but no hearts had been changed or feelings assuaged.

∫

Waits joined the women collecting bog berries. She had never known such despair. Returning from the judgment, her lodge members had found Thunder Sands dead by their lodge fire. Eagle Claw was now the acknowledged head of the lodge and she was his double-work mate. Claw was still recovering. Claw had not forced himself upon her yet, but the time was not far off. She cringed at the thought. She must find Love. She must tell him she would die for him, would wait forever for him, would....

"Curse you Waits! Do you think we all want to pick berries forever like dumb bears? Move it, fill your basket!" Tule Reed scolded Waits in her newfound role as Eagle's appointed overseer of her toil. Waits picked more berries, faster, for a while.

Waits was especially distracted because they were harvesting berries near the boggy lake where she had met Love. She kept looking for him in the bushes. There must be some way he would deliver her! He had not flinched as Claw's brand had burned his hand. He walked away from the judgment with honor, and looked at her with love and commitment as he departed. She knew he would save her. He must!

Some time later, she noticed it. If one were stooped over picking berries, one would not. In some of the far bushes, half-hidden by thick branches was an odd combination of pink, purple, and yellow. It was subtle and barely noticeable.

Waits noted where her fellow berry harvesters picked and then worked her way toward the colors without drawing attention to herself. Yes! It could only be Love!

The flower was one of the pink ones he had given her last spring, only this one was dried. The purple tree hair was only common in the oak grove by the lake bog. The yellow thing was one of the squishy round underground fleshes that popped out of the sand each late sun. Only Love would put them here together for her to find.

When she approached, she found an area of sand spread smooth, waiting for a message to be scratched. Waits didn't hesitate. She had been thinking about it for weeks and she must keep moving to avoid suspicion. She turned around and looked at her harvest mates as if she was squatting to pee. When she did squat, she quickly scratched a message. Four suns, and the hooded insect-eating plant that grew along the boggy margin of the lake. She rose and continued picking berries. If her harvest mates noticed anything, it was that she seemed to pick with more zeal after relieving herself. Be her odd behavior what it may, they thought of her.

∫

"Come to me!" Claw demanded. Waits obeyed. He lay on his furs and she sat next to him, hesitantly. Claw grabbed her and pulled her close, showing no respect or lodge decorum. He grunted rudely, "You are mine now. Let us see how you like my claw in your womb."

Waits could not deny him, but she could delay him. She leaned close to his ear.

"Blood on your slug?" she whispered insolently and vindictively.

Claw thrust her aside violently and denounced her for

all to hear, "Insult me if you wish, foul-mouthed womb woman, but you will bear my sons! Go cleanse yourself! Do it as often as you must! Do it well! Come back to me next week. You will be mine!" He turned over in his furs and shivered with anticipation, hidden weakness, and cold chills.

Later that evening, Waits told Tule Reed that her moon was full and asked if she could take away her red moss and cleanse herself. Her request to leave the lodge was routine. Tule hoped it would be the last such request for many years. Claw had strong seed.

Waits did not hesitate. All depended upon tonight. In the darkness she dashed among the dunes deep into the boglands, following memorized routes lit by glowing pathways. Dawn would come before long.

She flew into Love's arms. Thank Now he was here! He held her briefly and she felt his disfigured hand on her back. He pulled her away and looked into her eyes.

"My Love," she sighed.

"My Waits."

Waits wilted into his arms again and held him for some moments. Anguish flowed from her, into him, into their surroundings. Eventually she recovered, straightened, and gazed at Love once more. Then she dared.

"I am given to Claw-man. I cannot escape that fate. Nor can you. Not in this life."

Love watched her but did not respond.

Waits hesitated, looked down, regained her will, hugged Love again, and then returned her gaze to his face.

"What about lives to come?" She asked tenuously.

She saw the confusion in his eyes, then recognition of her idea, then enthusiasm, and finally caution.

Love thought for a long time. Waits waited.

Finally, he said, "Shall we live as long as your shaman so that we outlive the ones who curse us? Is this choice desirable, honorable and wise? Will it work?"

"Do you not love me forever?" she asked. She knew it was an unfair question. But, if he was unwilling to wait at least until Claw died, then his love might not be enduring enough for her to recover hope.

"I will love you forever. I will love you even when you are robbed of your maidenhood. I will love you through all time. Never will my love end. You are my maiden, whoever claims you or abuses you. I pledge my unending love for you. Until I die."

Love's vow of devotion made Waits dizzy. She felt overwhelming relief that they had not been put to death by her tribe. Who had ever heard such a proclamation of love? Her feelings towards Love Flames were reciprocal, but she had no voice to proclaim them.

She simply said, "Let us eat these jumpy ground-fleshes the bogman talked about." Maybe we will live forever. Claw will eventually die. I will then be yours after he passes, forever afterwards!"

They clasped each other and thought about it some more. Forever was a long time. Mistakes could linger. In the end, they both felt certain. They made their choice as one. Together they picked and ate the jumping ground-fleshes that Love had heard the shaman describe. Ignorant of how the true ritual worked, they chose the risks of immortality and unending love.

∫

Long Gull left his lodge well before dawn, sucking on yet another wad of pulverized willow bark crammed in his toothless mouth. Only one more time, he reflected. Then I can finally dispose of this useless, crippled, worn out body!

He had been drinking the stretch rot-flesh tea almost every day now, and the effect had almost entirely dissipated. What a waste. For a middle-aged body, a few cups of stretching tea could extend his health for many years. He had almost none left anyway. All that grew within walking distance he had collected last year and the new shelves grew very slowly.

Long Gull leaned on his trusty yew staff and hobbled along as best he could. Recent rains had increased the flow of the river so that canoeing upstream would be harder than walking. The rains also had brought out many of the other ground-fleshes that grew from the earth. He was almost certain the timing was right. The jumping ground-fleshes would be there and they would be fresh. Still, he needed to make sure before he brought Wave Eyes to the grove with him. The tribe might not give him a second chance to secret the boy away now that the lad was able to talk better and tell others what was going on. This would likely be his last visit to the grove before jumping. They had to be there. He must bring Wave Eyes tomorrow. He did not believe he would live even a few more weeks. The rains had come just in time. Soon he would be renewed!

After the long slow painful trek, Long Gull finally approached the grove as dawn's light started to permeate the world. Dense fog covered the lake and masked the grove. Only when he actually entered the grove did the tragic reality stab his eyes.

NOOO! NOOO! For the love of eternal NOWS, NOOO!

Long Gull slumped to the ground, his head drooped, and all his hopes fled. Waits for Love and her illicit suitor Love Flames lay jumbled together on the moss carpeting the floor of the grove. They were breathing, but they obviously did not inhabit their bodies. Only crumbs remained of the jumping ground-fleshes they had consumed. He looked around; maybe there were more. He found none; they had eaten the few that had appeared after the first early rain.

What were they thinking? Beyond Old groaned with dismay and growing anger. They did not know the ritual or the means of transference. Did they plan to jump into each other? What good would that do? Kneeling, he leaned back, lifted his face upwards, and howled his loss and rage to the uncaring sky. He felt life leaking away from this body he inhabited. They had doomed him. In his despair, born of long experience, he knew with certainty that he would not survive even the few more days until more of the jumping ground-fleshes came up. He would finally die.

His deep wisdom, distilled from countless lives, dispersed on the breezes of time and left only a cold stone of revenge. If he was to die, so would they. No! Worse! He would condemn them to live on without their bodies. His mind churned, ideas formed. He would also bind them to protect his people, his tribe, now that he no longer could.

Staggering to his feet, he lurched over to them and retrieved the few remaining scraps of the jumping ground-fleshes they had eaten. Loosening his spirit would help him cast his spell. He unceremoniously ate all the morsels he could find. Then he knelt by the body of Love Flames, took out the sharp knife he had used to cut off Eagle's arm, and slit the man's wrist. Blood flowed freely and soaked quickly through the moss into the sandy soil of the oak grove, nourishing entities that lived below ground. The body shuddered and flopped a few times weakly. The nearby spirit of Love Flames undoubtedly could sense what Beyond Old had done, but his body was too stupefied with the ground-fleshes for Love Flames to reoccupy and control it.

Next, he took Waits for Love's wrist in hand, but he just could not slice it. She was of the tribe. She was his offspring. He could not cut her. For a long time he moaned, frustrated in his plans. Finally, he realized he needed to dispose of their bodies anyway. The tribe must never know what had happened here. With waning strength, he stood and dragged Waits into the lake. Once she was in the water, he held her under to empty her breath. Suddenly, her eyes opened in terror and pierced him with frenzied panic. He felt like her spirit fingers were grabbing his mind, fighting back. Her body thrashed, but it had little strength and the movements were uncoordinated. The bubbles trailed off, her eyes grew dim, and then her movements stopped. He pushed her off into deeper water and watched her sink.

NO! How could I?

In his anger and dread, he had forgotten. For his incantation to work, their blood must mingle with the place where their bodies died. He stared abjectly at the now-still lake, crushed by his oversight. Then he noticed a red tinge stain the surface of the water. It came from below. Waits must have been in her moon. His relief was willful and callous.

Beyond Old almost couldn't extract his feet from the muck along the shore, but he finally managed to crawl to shore and also drag Love Flames' now bloodless body into the lake. He cast Love adrift into the lake also and watched him sink. All the elements of his bane were in place. Love's blood had soaked into the grove. Waits' was infusing the lake.

Beyond Old had used the jumping ground-flesh so many times, he was very sensitized to its effects. Already he could sense their spirits flailing at the edges of his consciousness. He was on the border of the in-between spirit realm where they were now trapped, indefinitely disembodied. He would lay his doom on them and then return to die a natural death, his spirit journeying on to the next realm.

Beyond Old gathered all his might, assessed all his loss, focused all his misery, and concentrated his love for his tribe. Then he walked the paths of power he had trod so often before. He confronted the spirits of the errant lovers and condemned them to protect his people and this place indefinitely. He bound them henceforth to this curst bog and baleful grove. Never shall they reincarnate until love released them and they were again needed in human form to further serve his tribe and this place. This was his doom. He compelled them to serve for unknown ages, always yearning for release. They would have ample time to consider their actions. They must wait.

With all the power of his hundred lives, he branded his curse immutably into the weft of reality, engendering melded sentiences comprised of their spirits, the bog, the grove, and the fleshes. The disembodied spirits of Waits and Love wailed their shock and disbelief. He felt no pity.

The effort had been so intense, that blood began to stream from his nose. Beyond Old turned his mind from the cursed spirits and tried to fully reinhabit his body. His spirit was still loose; the effects of the jumping ground-flesh remnants had not yet worn off. He noted his decrepit body was in deep water. His body's feet felt rooted in the sucking mud of the lake bottom. Water was near his body's nostrils. His body felt very cold and weak.

Chapter 10 — Sentience Chalices

He had never seen anything like it. They emerged through the swinging gymnasium doors and strutted forth like formidable forces of nature. He later compared them to a Richter 9 subduction zone quake shaking up their world and causing the resultant 500-year tsunami washing away all the community's old ideas and animosity.

Johnny and Grace were almost unrecognizable as they boldly strode down the middle isle of the auditorium, traversing the echoing gap of silence that Sheriff Ray's pistol had rent through the roar of the crowd. Johnny Wanders strode with boldness and courage; all traces of the hippy Indian kid had vanished. His posture was like a spear. His neat new dark green business suit contrasted stylishly with his proud black braid and a tie dotted with dark red cranberries. His demeanor was that of a brave warrior, an experienced victor of many battles with himself and others. Grace Flores swept along with confidence and purpose; she exuded a focused intent that no one had witnessed in her before. Her light river-blue dress was modern and elegant, and a lichen-patterned silk scarf was draped loosely over her shoulders. She seemed as sage and composed as a tribal elder exuding the wisdom of a thousand winters. No one but Johnny and Grace noticed, but Mary smiled slyly at them from her seat on the panel; she savored what was to come.

Few witnesses ever entirely agreed on what happened next. Many felt as if Johnny and Grace had entranced them, much like a mass hypnosis. The audacious twosome took to the stage and pronounced that neither of the development plans would proceed, that they had an alternative that would be far better for all concerned and for the land itself. Their brashness, certainty, and self-assurance floored the audience and muzzled the panelists. Even Stan was flummoxed.

For a period of time that might have comprised minutes or hours, Johnny and Grace presented their scenario to the audience as a fait accompli. They described the future so succinctly and forcefully that everyone imagined it was really just a very well articulated version of their own nascent ideas. The couple took turns portraying elements of their seamless vision, bouncing ideas back and forth off each other to build an edifice of inevitability.

Then, as a capstone to their exposition, they addressed every major stakeholder individually, and told each, very specifically, how they would benefit from the accord just described.

Ole had already settled on a single word for the best understatement of his life: "persuasive." Actually, their presentation was more like that science fiction book he had read about "memes," that is, infectious ideas that propagate on their own once released. The meeting broke up with "synergistic benefit" memes spreading like optimism viruses. Everyone waxed lyrical to each other about how they could become an integral part of this grand new project and they speculated about how their roles would benefit friends, families, and neighbors. The ramifications seemed endless; all possibilities enticed.

Without anyone noticing, Grace, Johnny and Mary calmly walked off the stage, exited a side door, and drove away in Grace's Prius. Shortly afterwards they had settled themselves within Mary's inner chamber in the back of Mysty Pages. Waits for Grace and Love Wanders had abided separation for an eternity, and for little time at all. Now their destined identities had commingled and they had their true names. They chose to delay just a little longer before officially consecrating their compounded love and devotion, especially now that they were confident that their simultaneously ancient and contemporary trysts would be honorably consummated. It would be a tremendously grateful, eagerly awaited and ardently reverential mating ceremony.

Mary had been digging deep into a pile of artifacts in a dusty corner and she finally excavated a leather box, which upon opening, revealed several items wrapped in animal furs.

"Here!" She proclaimed. "Talk about singular wine vintages. My grandmamaw gave me this special box when I was in my late twenties, shortly after our sole visit to the bog, and only a few months before she died. She said that I should keep the wine and the other enclosed items for a very special occasion. At the time, I could only wonder what she meant. Later, after I spawned Mysty Pages and set up my inner sanctum here, I examined and considered all the items again. Look." Mary handed the bottle to Johnny.

Grace snuggled close to him so they could both examine it. The bottle was squat, dark green, thick, and had bubbles in the glass. The cork looked like wood and it was sealed with red wax. The paper label was in surprisingly good condition, although it had a slight ridged pattern; probably it was handmade from cotton rag. The label also seemed to be hand-cut because the sides were not perfectly straight. What appeared to be glue stains showed through in light yellowish blotches along the edges and in a crosshatch mark in the middle. All the lettering was neatly hand-scribed with black ink in coarse block print. Below an enigmatic illustration, it read: "Tranebær (Craneberrie) Vin. Først crop. Nye var. Stankiewicz. Injun Picked. 1915 A.D. Olaf Görsman, Prop."

Although the languages and spelling were jumbled and semiliterate, the meaning was clear enough. Above the lettering, the sketch consisted of puzzling doodle marks, not at first recognizable. The markings appeared to be charcoal rather than ink. Then the strokes fell into place for both of them. Olaf might have made the wine, but a native had done the sketch. Maybe even Mary's greatmamaw? The stylized etching undoubtedly depicted a bog, a grove, and twin spirits. There was also a faint squiggle off to one side. They looked at each other and shuddered.

Mary reached out her hand. "What better time to open it?" They could not have agreed more and passed the bottle back to her. Mary eventually resorted to her Swiss army knife to extract the stubborn wood stopper. She sniffed the opened bottle and a smile lit her face.

"Smells dry and tart! Ol' Olaf, Bert, n' Ole have always

known how to make cranbalicious wine!"

Only the most exceptional drinking vessels would do for this occasion. Mary poured the wine into two carefully shaped and intricately carved goblets made from the cranial bones of the skull of an infant grey whale.

"Pre-settlement," she told them as she poured, "but that's a whole 'nother story."

Awed but focused, Johnny lifted his goblet towards Waits. "To a long wander for perfect love."

Beyond overwhelmed, Grace lifted her goblet towards Love. "To perfect love that ripens with long waiting."

Talk about immeasurable understatements, thought Mary. She just savored the moment. Then they both looked at her in anticipation. Waits for Grace handed Mary her chalice. Tears flowed in rivulets down both of Mary's cheeks, like the Wayward River overflowing both banks. She lifted the goblet and said, "To our future."

Each recalled the toasts as memorable.

∫

B-Bob (boisterous Bob Newall), officially nominated Master of Introductions for the evening, bellowed, "Please join me in expressing our gratitude and respect to the two individuals, without whom this evening would never have occurred, Johnny Wanders and Grace Flores!"

The assembled diners rose to their feet and responded with raucous approval. The couple got up from their table in front and bounded onto the stage waving their hands. More than one person in the crowd noted they appeared as

Talk about immeasurable understatements, thought Mary.

youthful as they had on that memorable evening twelve years ago. The community now revered them almost as the Greeks did their gods and goddesses, so perhaps lingering youth was appropriate.

It took minutes of smiling, waving, and waiting for the crowd to quiet enough for them to speak. When they did, their voices came across crystal clear because the spacious new conference/dining/meeting facility had a small flock of state-of-the-art RoTees.

The semi-acronym "RoTees" was a thankfully shortened and easy to pronounce version of "rotorized robotic telephonic and telescopic recorders." These inconspicuously small devices were networked, AI-controlled, and capable of flittering around near the ceiling on tiny mechanical wings. By doing so, they were able to simultaneously record the high-resolution images and sounds (especially voices) of several people or tableaus at once. They did so from multiple perspectives and could very quickly switch between objects of attention or viewpoints. To enhance the fun, the controlling AI chose which recordings to instantly replay on several conference room screens....

Johnny dove right in. "Thank you, Bob, and thank you all so much! I can't tell you what a pleasure it is for Grace and me to be here with you all to celebrate the 10th anniversary of BogLand!" Johnny hardly got the words out before more waves of handclapping and whooping forced him to pause again.

"Thank you! Thank you everyone," Grace continued. "Johnny and I want to make sure that each and every one of you knows that none of this would have happened without your inspiration and hard work!"

Programmed to boost the volume a bit after introductory applause, the RoTees' sound system started compensating and allowed the speakers to continue before the second wave of clapping fully faded, thus inconspicuously preserving the momentum of the presentations and excitement of the evening's events.

"Tonight we have planned a twofold ceremony," Johnny carried on. "Not only will we honor all those who made this possible, but we will celebrate our accomplishments publicly. Conducting her first official major ceremony on our behalf, please thank our Public Relations Coordinator, Maybelle Tattleton…." Johnny paused only momentarily to let the gaggle quickly get in their hoots.

"Maybelle has returned to us after nearly completing her Master's in Public Relations at the University of Oregon. Her thesis project is designing, planning, and implementing this evening's anniversary celebration. Her integrated RoTee netcast, holodoc, and archvinterp package will let the world know about our successes, encourage new visitors, and save the proceedings for posterity! Thanks Maybelle!"

About half the RoTees focused on Maybelle from a variety of angles to ensure hi-res 3D modeling of her beet-red blush, starting the auto-collection of peak moment snippets.

"We created BogLand together, so we will celebrate each other," Grace continued, "We will pass introductions like a relay. So have a seat and let yourselves digest that fabulous feast we have just completed. A refreshing dessert will be served shortly. Meanwhile, sip and savor the fine Oregon wines that are being served and join us in commemorating the BogLand's 10th anniversary!"

"To get started," Johnny picked up the pace, "I have fabulous news. Among our guests tonight is Oregon's newly elected governor, Jeff Atkins. Give him a hand folks!"

Jeff stood and bowed several times to the crowd's noisy admiration, but then sat again. "Jeff has declined to speak tonight, insisting that this night is for us to celebrate. Jeff is more than a modest public servant, he is a statesman!" More cheers.

"The exciting news for us is that Jeff told us over dinner tonight that he is appointing our very own Grace Flores as Commissioner of the state Office of Community Development and Nature Conservation! Let's give her a big round of applause!"

This time half the RoTees converged on Grace's face. Her smile was radiant and the crowd (both in-flesh and televirtual) sighed at her serene beauty. Starting then, and during the course of the entire evening, the peak moment snippet folders and other docufiles would resize themselves several times over to accommodate the frequent high points, dramas, and resultant holobytes.

Johnny bowed to Grace with histrionic flair and a melodramatic swirl of his hand.

Grace laughed merrily and turned to the audience.

"Thanks Johnny," she replied with exaggerated, pseudo-mock gratitude.

"Just over a decade ago," she recalled, "our community was rife with dissension about development plans. Now

BogLands is a model admired and emulated by communities around the world. YOU did it, but the leadership of Johnny Wanders has been fundamental to our success!" Grace waited for the ovation to diminish and for people to take their seats again.

"As CEO of BogLand, the South Coast's premier resort, education, and entertainment complex, his enthusiasm and long-term vision have guided us down a path of synergistic opportunities rarely encountered in community development and nature conservation. Thank you, Johnny!" With that, Grace stepped off the stage and shared hugs and handshakes on the way back to her seat.

"Next, it is my great pleasure," Johnny pressed on, "to welcome the honorable head of the Confederated Tribes of the Sand Coast, BogLands board member, and its Director of Tribal Culture, Wally One-Path Jackson! Come on up, Wally."

While the big man got to his feet and ascended the stage, Johnny continued, "Wally has been a true inspiration to our entire enterprise. BogLands would not be the success it is today without the close collaboration we have built with the Confederated Tribes of the Sand Coast. They have provided the best possible location for our complex, here on their short strip of land along Highway 101. Proximity to several cranberry farms and natural bogs has allowed us to create a multifaceted education and entertainment experience for our visitors, while minimizing our ecological footprint because this small area was already cleared for development several decades ago. Our native brand of cranberry products is rapidly becoming renown. You will hear more about that soon. Here's Wally!"

"Thanks, thank you all." Wally waited. "I am not a fancy speaker, so I will just tell you the story of BogLand through my eyes. When I first tried to convince our newly formed confederation that we needed a casino, it was because I believed we needed it to survive. But, I had also visited other tribal casinos. They seemed to be full of dead souls. No one was having fun. There were no smiles. Flashing lights could not hide the gloom. Before BogLand, I accepted the notion that we must operate such a place just to exist. My thoughts were too small. All our thoughts were too small. We ... you and me, the tribe and the community ... we have created here a new story, a new way of thinking, a way founded on respect."

Wally had become known as a soft-spoken, thoughtful leader over the last decade, and the gathered celebrants were listening carefully to his considered observations and opinions. "We have created the means to seamlessly combine business, games, recreation, relaxation, healthy products, tribal heritage, local history, education, art, and nature conservation. Moreover, we have had one heck of a lot of fun doing it!"

"Jah, ya could say dat," Bugs observed with a quiet smirk to himself from near the front as Wally paused, but a roving RoTee caught and amplified his comment. Another synced RoTee flashed in telefocus and caught the legendary twinkle in Bugsy's eye to add a visual to the "understatement snippets" they had been programmed to capture.

Chuckling as he continued, "I will let others talk about the projects they coordinate, but I must say, we do not operate a 'casino.' Our gaming facilities are like no others.

We have no-wager games tailored for players that range from toddlers to elders. Each is exciting, educational, and full of intrigue. Each game exhibits Native American, coastal nature, or cranberry themes. I think my favorite is watching kids play, 'Sing like a Whale'."

"We also have games that do entail wagers, but unlike other casinos, these emulate native games of chance, stimulate development of new skills, and involve odds that only slightly favor the house. Nobody loses big, no one gets addicted to the false notion they are going to get rich, and everyone has fun. Even our virtual hand-guess game is a lot better than yanking on one-armed bandits! Who woulda thunk it? Our BogLand Complex earns almost as much money per square foot as many casinos because we are family friendly! Even big Las Vegas boys are investigating our success," Wally paused, "and they spend a lot of their money here when they visit to experience our operation first hand…" he wound down to more laughter.

Wally raised his hand to call for quiet and announced, "Would my dear aunt and revered tribal elder Mary Duneflower Jackson please join me on the stage?" Mary, looking very regal, and simultaneously not a little silly in her over-the-top native attire, sauntered onto the stage with a gleam in her eye. Mary never took herself too seriously, but she took others' concerns very seriously. That is why she was universally adored. Wally gave her a big hug. Her short stature and her colorful feathers, furs, leathers, cloths, and shell jewelry contrasted outlandishly with tall husky Wally in his tailored cowboy suit, rattlesnake skin boots, and Stetson hat. Another snippet.

"Mary has done more to resurrect and perpetuate our

tribal heritage than anyone could possibly have imagined. Where she gets her insights, wisdom and knowledge is anyone's guess. She will only say that her grandmamaw and greatmamaw taught her a lot, she reads avidly, and she listens closely to the land. Even so, one would think she was making up half of it, were it not for the fact that what she teaches rings so true in the hearts of our tribal members. Somehow she has practically resurrected our ancient languages and fifteen young children now take instruction. Elders and teachers from other tribes come to consult with her. Anthropologists and archeologists request interviews and consultations. Linguists record her talking our native tongues and investigate her language skills in detail. She wins each of their hearts and invites them to help us continually improve our Native Heritage Center which draws visitors from around the world. Please help me show our appreciation for Mary's efforts on our behalf!" They did, loudly.

Everyone expected Mary to stand stoically looking at them, one by one, until the room eventually quieted. Mary never had liked being predictable though. Little known to most, she practiced doing something differently every day. Flexibility was the essence of youth in her book. Anyway, she was enjoying herself far too much tonight. She took a clue from Bugsy and surrendered herself to a little impishness. With a flourish, she jumped in the air, landed stomping her feet in a quick native rhythm dance, sing-sang a hee haw haw, twirled to show off, in full splendor, her thrown-together inner sanctum costume, jerked to a frozen crouch facing the audience, lifted her left palm towards them, and shouted "YAI!" Had they not already been focused on her, she would have been too fast for the RoTees. They still had not responded fast enough to maximize resolution and optimize view angles. The stunned audience reacted even more slowly. Mary took pity on them. So she stood normally again, acted as if nothing terribly unusual had happened, and said, "Sorry folks, just wanted to liven things up a bit." Nervousness morphed into appreciative twitters as people regained their trust in Mary's underlying sanity. Those who knew her best were suffused with mirth.

Mary started pacing back and forth, speaking as she went, intentionally testing the coordination, program priorities, aim, and auto-focus capabilities of the RoTees. "Seriously though, folks, I could not have accomplished any of what Wally went on about without the generous help of countless friends and colleagues.

"Our heritage and interpretation activities are threefold. I've coordinated the tribal library, museum, and art gallery; Sally Gorseman, among her other duties, does the same for the cranberry cultivators theme; and Twarn Thongchai has headed up the nature program. Outside assistance has poured in like a flood. Why? I'd say it's our joint vision; that is, a communal purpose rooted in the bogs, the dunes, and the ancestral spirits themselves. Nothing motivates like a common goal. Nothing draws aid like a clear path forward and confident people trodding it."

The crowd, Mary thought, was listening too soberly to her insights; thus, spinning around again, she lightened it up. "So check it out! Our museum displays change monthly. I am always adding new books to our library and the store. The schedule of our educational events is displayed in front of the museum, printed in the newsletter, and posted online. Be there or miss out. Join us. Learn, teach, and grow. Thanks!"

"Now, enough of tribes, let's talk CRANBERRIES!"

"Yahoo!" belted out Jake Booley, who had been power-sipping a little too much wine, and did his own little seated shindig at his table. Jake was moving slowly enough that his embarrassing performance was recorded from start to sloppy finish in high-res 3D, and in four-part harmony, as Arlo would have put it. No matter. Jake was widely liked too, and his stunt provided another comic interlude.

"So OLE! Get your beautiful Nordish behind up here lad!" Mary belted. Had he had more practice at eye rolling, he would have spun them in his sockets. He didn't though, so Ole just shucked his shoulders and modestly climbed onto the stage. "Folks," Mary spoke forcefully into the chortling din created by Jake, "please welcome the marketing director for our new line of cranberry products.

"Ole has single-handedly transformed run of the mill south coast cranberries and juices into the NOW Berry brand! Our Native, Organic, and Wholesome array of cranberry products will soon overtake Ocean Spritz in brand recognition. Mark my words! Nowww… here's Ole!"

Ole looked at the huge circle of friends, and said, "Thank you."

Ole looked directly at Mary. The RoTees spun into innovation mode and difocused.

"I am honored that the Confederated Tribes of the Sand Coast have graciously chosen to create this innovative and profitable coalition with the local cranberry farmers and our community to market premium grade NOW cranberries. I ask you all to stand and join me in officially honoring the Tribes with our show of appreciation."

Given the standing ovation inside, nobody noticed the growing thunderstorm outside. The atmosphere was electric, almost cathartic. The commotion receded and Mary spoke again.

"I constantly tell people that cranberries were considered a gift of peace by Native Americans. How fitting it is that the dessert now being served consists of our scrumpdeli-icious frozen native cranberries, drizzled with a little cream from naturalized European cows, and sweetened with the honey of trust and cooperation. Give thanks and enjoy. Peace!" At that, Mary returned to her seat and Ole continued.

"Peace and NOW," Ole reflected aloud, "it almost sounds 'Ram Dassian. Well, why not? Even better, our NOW brand is selling products like crazy! Talk about 'value added.' Buyers are going wild over the fact that our cranberries are of the very highest quality. We 'dry-harvest' our cranberries. Our skilled and well-paid laborers, many tribal members included, handpick them, one by one, rather than floating away all the berries, of whatever quality, in a murky soup of irrigation water and berm critter droppings. Then we painstakingly high-grade the crop to select only the best berries. Our farmers take pride in abiding by organic and salmon-friendly certification guidelines; indeed, they enjoy the challenge of pioneering innovative means to improve the eco-friendliness of cranberry cultivation. The net result is that we have circumvented the economic incentive to convert more natural bogs and wetlands to bulk cranberry cultivation."

Ole paused to remember the end of his speech. "I might be called the Marketing Director but the NOW Berry brand of cranberry products is selling itself. Not only do they taste superb, but our top quality berries are also jam-packed with health benefits. We are selling this delicious wholesomeness in a wide variety of value-added products. All with the berry over the bog NOW logo Annie Kirkpatrick devised for us!"

"Before I pass on this 'preaching to the choir' road show," Ole said, "I want to acknowledge several individuals that made all this possible. I couldn't convince them to climb up on stage, but they will find out that they are on stage anyway. Did they really think they could avoid Maybelle's technologically-enhanced talents?"

"First let's give a big round of thanks to Bugsy Sopp, the President of the new Sand Coast Cranberry Farmers Association, formed by the old CFA and the tribe. The acronym, SCCFA, still doesn't do much for me, but hey, it is what it is. Bugs has guided and inspired all the farmers participating in our association with his foresight and amicable humor! Bugs, stand up and take a bow!"

Bugs felt he had been preempted by Mary's little dance on stage and Jake's seat jiggle, but he would have plenty of opportunities to rib them about that later. He restrained himself to a moderate jig and an elaborate 360 degree bow. Snippet.

"And Hector." Ole continued from the stage, "Folks, I want you to know that my former farm manager has contributed to all our good fortunes many times over. Without him as labor manager for the SCCFA, our coordinated enterprise would not be where it is. He values labor and laborers value him. Our farmers rely on his program to provide a steady supply of trained and motivated workers. To do so, he has developed a comprehensive plan for our work force. It includes a fair package of training, pay, and benefits combined with performance incentives. State bureaucrats and farm labor representatives have visited to find out how he designed such an effective package. I call it respect and common sense. Please, join me in extending our thanks to Hector Hernandez!"

The RoTees only caught a brief "Gracias" as Hector modestly bowed once.

"Now I have the exquisite privilege of passing the emcee baton to my wife and love of my life, the Managing Director for BogLand, ladies and gentlemen, please welcome, Sally Darlington-Gorseman!"

"Sally might once have been merely, 'vun fine and vivacious country gal,' to quote my old buddy Bugs, but she is now the driving executive force behind Oregon's most emulated tourist destination."

Thrilled, Sally jumped onto the stage and planted a kiss on her shy husband that was so ardent it almost fried the RoTees' electronics. A new archvinterp category was auto-created and the online audience buzzed with delight.

Ole seemed dazed as he stumbled off the stage. Sally stepped front and center, raised her hand in pride, and shouted, "BogLand NOW!" A few seats were overturned and many tables jostled as the diners surged to their feet and returned the cry and salute.

The tinkle of a few breaking wine glasses convinced the waiting staff that it was time to slow the serving of wine, even though many bottles remained unopened. The table busing staff incrementally notched up its clearing pace a tad, focusing first on rounding up the shards. Few in the audience paid them any mind as they settled down to listen to Sally.

"I can't thank you all enough," she began, "but there still remain hidden among you bashful people who do deserve public appreciation.

"First, I want to thank Twarn Thongchai!" Hoots from the audience included "Shrum-Dude!," "My Thai Man," and "MycoMystery Tour," each accolade relished by mini-segments of the more eccentric online viewer clicks. Twarn was held in high esteem by the local gathering too.

"Twarn has single-handedly transformed a portion of the tribe's bogs, wetlands, forests, dunes, and beachfront into a fabulous nature interpretation experience for young and old, nimble and alter-abled. For the brief, lazy, or jaded visitor, nearly every natural vegetation feature found on the reservation has been incorporated into the landscaping around the resort. From there on out, it only gets better. Twarn has designed and organized a diverse array of guided nature walks for our guests. Indeed, his silent electric dune buggy excursions down the old right of way are creating quite the buzz. He also facilitates statewide field ecology tours, seminars, and retreats for K-12 through university classes. Researchers, ranging in expertise from interns to prominent scientists, study and teach here.

"OK," Sally waved her hands to suppress the crowd's increasing murmurs, "the activity for which Twarn is most esteemed just happens to be his MycoTours. I am endlessly flabbergasted at how much Asian and European tourists will pay to join Twarn on one of his exclusive mushroom hunting expeditions among the wild parts of the Tribes' inner reservation lands. Our premier chefs, that same evening, prepare mushrooms that the participants have picked that day. Those dishes have evoked fits of epicurean ecstasy the likes of which I have never before witnessed. To Twarn's credit, after expenses and his own modest wages, he insists that all the proceeds from this endeavor go to the needy and struggling in our community, especially children. He says he is inspired by his own childhood. We can't thank you enough, Twarn. Please take a bow!"

Twarn stood, and emulating other putatively bashful audience virticipants, raised a fresh primo specimen of *Tricholoma magnivelare* over his head to thank the species, lowered it to his nose, took a big sniff, and collapsed into his chair with a vaudevillian display of olfactory delirium. Hilarity ensued. Snippets.

"Next, I want to honor the 180-degree Man!" Sally vocalized loudly to cut through the din and move things along.

Stan had earned his nickname from his sincere come-about, and he loved the descriptive moniker. Where he had once used 'greenness' to cover his greed, he was now a true believer, one of the most prominent promoters of renewable energy on the south coast. "Born again," one might say, and some had, accurately.

"Mr. Stanley C. Latterly has ensured that BogLand is not only energy self-sufficient, but that we contribute electricity to the grid. In cooperation with the Tribe and Oregon State University, we have installed cutting-edge wave energy generators just offshore. We have also installed geothermal heat pumps and covered every roof in our compound with highly efficient solar panels. Stan is exporting our design concepts for extreme efficiency and local energy throughout a region too harshly criticized for its gloomy weather. Well phooey on such naysayers! Stan has shown that with innovative financing, these measures can be cost effective even without public funds. Yeah, Stan!"

Stan rarely did anything half-assed nowadays, including his wardrobe. He had a new motto. Life was for fun, so do good things boldly and enjoy yourself! He stood, flaunting his spring-green organic cotton suit, tipped his solar panel cowboy hat, and formally bowed. Every observer ate it up.

"We sing Stan's praises now, and so we should, but it was Donny boy who egged him on! Let's hear it now for that wannabe old-country codger, Don Kirkpatrick and his Leprechaun Transportation Hub!"

Don stood, (no Roman vin fer him) an' den hae hefted de Guinness he were trinkin' up te de blokes n' lasses, and den hae toasted "Haers te yaell!" or some such blarney. The AI translation program struggled.

"There is no other destination resort," Sally plowed on, "where visitors are required to park their private cars during their stay. Nor is there any comparable example where they want to do so. Don has designed an all-electric walkway, auto-rickshaw, coach-buggy, shuttle, and trolly transport system that seamlessly handles every contingency from baggy people to people's baggage. While you visit, you can recharge your electric vehicle directly from the station's grid. You can also fill up with any combination of gasoline, diesel, bioethanol, or biodiesel you desire. Just pluck the four-leafed holoclover, and you are home free. Thank you Don!

"Next, let's all groove on the power of image. Oooommmmmm. Yes, you heard it from me! Mrs. Annie Kirkpatrick has booted our ideas into the realm of eye-catchin', attention-hookin', logos, themes and signs. She has worked with each of us to transform our creative notions into unforgettable mass perceptions. I bow to you, imagination goddess!"

The wall behind Sally segued through a series of Annie's logos and themes as she spoke. HoloVirt chatroom visitors discussed their originality and impact.

"My personal favorite is the Mypps weather board!"

The number and diversity of popular weather phrases and acronyms shouted from the audience were too varied for the RoTees to parse and categorize; only a subset were accessioned. "Annie, Bonny, and Holly are primarily responsible for one of the most popular insta-weather cipher systems on the West Coast. Yippie! Thank you!"

Holly stood up, the RoTees zoomed, and she formally portended, "It's swiftly approaching category D&D; that is, 'dunder n' discord,' outside. Ya'll might wanta prep yourselves for some atmospheric discontent." Holly seemed a might tipsy, hence her advice was noted, but foolishly ignored by most. Not Sally.

"Right! I have just a few more people I want to recognize, and then we have some music and dancing planned, but if anyone wants to leave and try to beat the impending storm, feel free." Who was she kidding? She noted not a single person made a move to go, even though her offer was immediately bolstered by another loud crack of thunder.

"Okay, then," she persevered, "First I want you all to give a big round of thanks to my good friend and trusted matchmaker, Bonny Sopp, for this fabulous banquet." Continuing through the din, "After buckling down in mid-life to earn a degree in Food Services Management from OSU, Bonny has excelled as our culinary coordinator for BogLand. She oversees catered events, fine romantic dining, family dining, a 24-hour casual food bar, and a wide selection of healthy snacks. Of course, our NOW cranberries are prominently featured among many of the delicious and nutritious offerings, as are Twarn's sopps seasonally. Thanks, Bonny!

"And, Gabriella Hernandez has just completed the online Facilities Management Certificate Program offered by the University of Washington. Beginning this month, she assumes the role of BogLand Lodgings Manager. She will be overseeing accommodations that range from luxury and bridal suites, to comfortable hotel rooms, to cottages, cabins, yurts, and even a tent campground. We all look forward to Gabriella doing for BogLand hospitality what Hector has done for our cranberry farms labor force. Congratulations Gabriella!

"Finally, I want to praise the generous political support that County Commissioner Ray Wilson has heaped on our endeavors, and the "Got Security?" education program that Sheriff Billy Anders has helped us design and institute. Greatly appreciated guys!

"The last and dearest person I want to thank before we get to the evening's entertainment is my darling mom! I believe that each and every person who has ever visited us has commented on how much they like the coastal "Flotsam and Jetsam" decoration theme that distinguishes our landscaping and adorns our buildings. I never believed the collection at the entrance to mom's driveway could be outdone, but she has attracted donors to BogLand's eccentric assemblage of coastal curiosities like zucchini growers to a gleaner's market. After we skim off the best to display around the property, items still fly out of the gift shop faster than they can be collected off the beach or produced by local artisans. Thank you Holly!

"Now, I would like to hand the evening over to Bogland's events coordinator, Bob Wilkens. Take it away, Bob!"

Speakers were now encountering serious competition from the incessant rumbling thunder. Can the band play louder than the storm? He wondered as he took the stage. Will I ever be heard clearly? His self-pity was endearing to those who knew him best.

"Thanks Sally, and thank you B-Bob, Grace, Johnny, Wally, Mary, Ole, and Sally for this rousing anniversary ceremony!

"It ... CRACK ... is now my ... BOOM ... pleasure to announce ... RUMBLE ... our newly reconstituted community dance band," he tried valiantly to communicate, "the Boggy Bottom Gagglers!"

Just as the band was striking up their first song, dual lightning bolts jumped upwards from the artificial bogs on both sides of the conference hall and stabbed the lolling clouds. The shafts of withering electricity twined around each other like a DNA helix and their feet danced across BogLand's solar panel arrays with an intensity born from eons of avoided doom. The discharge surged through the grid inverter boxes and fried every electronic component in the entire complex. EM pulses even scrambled the stasis memory of everyone's portable electronic devices. The insect-mimic RoTees spat sparks as they fluttered to the floor, leaving optic trails in the sudden darkness. The backup lock-storage organo-memory matrices melted and all the local recordings of the evening's events dissipated into entropic back-eddies.

Other than temporary ear ringing, no person was hurt and no panic ensued. The wine had been too good and they were having too much fun sharing the pregnant moments of an outrageous now. The storm passed almost as quickly as it had swept down on them. Everyone left calmly, satiated with the evening's repast, reveling in a wealth of memories, and appreciative of the firmament's dynamite dunder n' discord show.

Maybelle, of course, was very bummed that her public relations thesis project had been so capriciously zapped by forces beyond her control. Even state of the art media facilities and equipment, it seemed, were susceptible to damage by extreme voltaic discharges. When repairs were finally made and Maybelle got back online, she was able to piece together a fairly complete record of the evening's events from snippets and youtubules that virticipants had autoglommed from the cloud. Unfortunately, the resolution of such retro-data was correspondingly low.

There also seemed to be a curious pattern of gaps in content. She had been synchromonitoring all the recordings of the RoTees in real time, both onstage and among audience members. Compared to her memory, she now found no instances among the extant recordings of things she had noted previously, such as phrases like "lingering youthfulness," or "ancestral spirits." Nor did she note any mention of Mary's amazing tribal knowledge, wild parts of the reservation, or the natural bogs. Way atypical, Maybelle thought briefly, but then the anomalies soon slipped from her mind as she focused on piecing together the scavenged remnants of her thesis.

∫

"I never asked, what did happen when you called me from the berm?"

Ole surfaced from his revelry, "Huh?"

"Come on, you know, when you called on your cell phone to ask me to the Cranberry Festival, lo those many years ago. What happened to Bugsy that interrupted the call?"

Ole finally caught up to Sally's train of thought. A mind reader he wasn't. "Oh, that," he said. Walking along the berm dividing his old Stankovich berry bogs should have suggested to him the context of Sally's query.

"What's she talking about Ole?" Grace inquired. "Did it have something to do with my hubby's notorious bog incident?" She was holding Johnny's arm as they walked along, and she looked at him as she asked Ole.

"No, no," Ole responded, "this was several days after Johnny had trespassed to our mutual embarrassment. Bugs and I were taking an evening stroll along this very berm. He kept bugging me about the apparition I had seen when confronting Johnny, so to distract him from his interrogation, I asked if he thought I should take Sally to the Cranberry Festival. Bugs got so excited about the prospect, that he convinced me to call Sally on the spot with my cell phone. Just as Sally picked up and we started to chat, Bugs got down on his hands and knees and started examining the footprints left that fateful night by Johnny, me, and the gaggle of giggling high school girls."

Turning from Grace and Johnny to Sally, Ole continued, waving his arms to illustrate, "So anyway, Bugs was snooping along the ground as we talked, and all of the sudden he ended up face to face with a nutria that was cowering in its burrow. It was threatened, I suppose, because the critter lunged at Bugsy and bit him on the nose. Bugs stumbled backwards and landed on his butt. Then, I tripped over Bugsy and tried not to land on that huge rat. I lost my balance in the scuffle, the cell phone went flying, I rolled over, caught it in mid-air, and then, well, it took me a little while to stop laughing. Sorry," he ended sheepishly.

Sally smiled appreciatively at his gesticulating rendition of the event and hooked his arm. The two couples strolled slowly toward the western wall, enjoying the warm ocean breeze, the scent of millions of cranberry flowers, and the splendor of a lingering spring day.

Approaching the barrier, Johnny asked, "How's the fence working out, or should I call it The Great Green Wall of the West?"

Ole harrumphed, "Jah, you might call it that. I still have to shake my head at how long it took to convince Bugsy that his spooky ghost stories about an Alluring Bog Maiden would be counterproductive for the purpose of keeping out the tourists.

"Actually, the wall seems to be working as planned. Bugs now tells me that very few people on the cranberry farm tours even ask about it. When someone does, Bugs usually just tells the group that it is meant to keep bears from eating the berries. Most tourists are clueless and enjoy the humor in that unlikely fiction. A few see through his pat response and are more persistent about the probability of bears getting in from other directions if they so desired. Then Bugsy just tells them a part of the truth; that BogLand doesn't want its visitors trampling over some portions of the reservation that are set aside for customary tribal rituals. That seems to satisfy most everyone. He never mentions the very special bog and grove behind this wall, or that it remains part of my farm."

"Speaking of which," Johnny noted, "I think our lawyers have all the details of the conservation easement worked out. The tribal council simply has to vote on the motion that we have already negotiated and then authorize expenditure of the funds."

"Great!" Ole and Sally responded simultaneously.

Only 10 years of marriage, and they were already speaking with one mind, Johnny grinned to himself. "With the way BogLand is going, it shouldn't be too long before we can allocate enough money to buy your back forty outright. That is, if you two or your heirs," he looked significantly at Sally's expanding abdomen, "still chose to sell."

"I see no reason why we wouldn't," Ole replied, "that bog rightfully should be entrusted to the Confederated Tribes. We just want a little nest-eggs for the tadpoles." Sally swerved aside and made a show of not letting Ole pat her belly as he said that. She would break him yet of using that term for the budding offspring she nurtured!

Just then, the gate in the wall opened from the inside, and out came the two biologists. They were laden with gear and looked anxious to leave. Amy appeared a might pale, Grace thought. A little concerned, she stepped forward to greet them. "Hi Amy and Chad. Is everything alright?"

Although they both seemed distracted, Amy answered. "I think we're done."

"Super," Grace said and then looked around. "Does everyone know each other here?"

Amy said, "I met Ole the day we made arrangements, but otherwise no." Chad just grunted as he fussed over some device.

Grace made introductions. "This is Johnny Wanders, my husband and CEO of Bogland and this is Sally, Ole's wife and Managing Director. Johnny, Sally, this is Amy Whitam, forest mycologist with Oregon State University and Chad Gurtney, a rare species propagator and former colleague of mine with the Conservancy." Amy was polite enough to shake hands, but Chad only managed to nod as he kept fiddling with his GPS unit.

"So, anyway, this should be our last trip," Amy volunteered, "I think we got the last of the samples we need." She still seemed preoccupied, however.

Grace filled in for her. "Amy and Chad have spent several years now propagating the rare species found in and around the bog and transplanting them to other appropriate habitats along this section of the coast. Some of those boggy habitats are on public lands and some are on private lands where the Conservancy is negotiating easements for their protection. The hardest thing to propagate has been those Amanita mushrooms, right?"

Amy nodded and unenthusiastically launched into an abbreviated version of her rote research explanation spiel. "Yes, many ectomycorrhizal species of fungi are difficult to inoculate onto tree roots from their spores. Similarly, pure mycelial extracts cultured from sporocarps or their mycorrhizal mantles grow very slowly in pure culture. Inoculation of new plant roots from such cultures present significant challenges. My graduate students and I, however, have developed a technique to procure micromycelial fragments from the interior Hartig net of mycorrhized root tips and insert those cellular fungal fragments directly into the root tip cortex of aseptically grown tree seedlings. This works better than inoculations with other fungal culturing and inoculation methods because fungal cells excised from from the cortex of an original mycorrhizal root tip are already epigenetically activated for the physiological exchanges required to rapidly establish new mutualistic symbioses with the appropriate host."

Okaaay....Ole and Sally thought to themselves and waited for her to finish. Johnny had a clearer notion of what she meant, but from a different perspective. He was not about to share his experience with this group.

"From acorns collected in this grove, Chad has grown some sizable, and still sterile, three year-old oak seedlings. The ectomycorrhizal root tips I collected today should allow us to extract distinct cortical hyphal cells to inoculate them with our target fungus. Hopefully, in a few years, we will be transplanting offspring of the grove oaks, along with their newly described *Amanita jumpponi* fungal symbionts, to other dune wetland sites.

"Where did you come up with that species name anyway, Grace?" Amy asked in a offhanded manner.

"It was just such a gas finding them, you know, like the Rolling Stones' Jumpin' Jack Flash lyrics," Grace lied, "or like they will be jumping to new habitats."

"Right," Amy doubted aloud. "And the *Echinodontium stretchii*?"

Grace smiled and was ready to dissemble again when...

"Damn!" Chad cursed. Then he looked up. "Oh, sorry. I just can't get this blankety-blank GPS unit to latch onto any satellites. I thought it was the grove canopy or the wall back there, but we are out in the open now. For that matter," he looked at the four of them almost accusingly, "I can never seem to get clear satellite imagery of the bog from Google Earth or any other resource mapping program!"

Everyone let him stew for a few moments, and then Grace calmly reminded him, "I believe you will recall, in our memorandum of understanding, that the location of this bog was not to be revealed."

"I know, but it was only for my own records!" Chad defended himself.

"I am sorry your equipment seems to be malfunctioning. It must be fun to use and a valuable aid in remote places. I think you can probably describe the location well enough from your current records, though," she suggested carefully. Continuing honestly, "Anyway, I want you both to understand that you have our enduring gratitude for all the fabulous work you have done. We all tremendously appreciate how much you have contributed to ensure the survival of these ultra-rare organisms." Johnny, Ole, and Sally expressed their agreement as they all shook hands goodbye.

Chad still seemed agitated. Ole thought he heard him mutter something under his breath about being glad to never visit that creepy bog again as he departed. Amy's hurried pace suggested she agreed.

∫

The summer solstice was only a couple of weeks away and the sun slid diagonally across the low western sky as dusk gradually approached. A toasty fire was crackling in the stone ring they had laid near the grove and bog for their private anniversary picnics. Over the last couple of hours, they had leisurely enjoyed a simple but delicious meal, some fine wine, and relaxed conversation. Now each couple snuggled and their thoughts turned inwards.

Ole considered himself the luckiest man in the world, and soon to be a father to boot! Sally had transformed his comfortable but routine existence into one of love, joy, daily surprises and nonstop challenges. There was no end in sight. What more could a man ask?

Early in their marriage, Sally had struggled to stop comparing her devoted new husband with the self-centered jerk she had originally married. But, she had transcended the trauma of her divorce years ago and was now flowering as a person. Much of this change resulted from the confidence he showed in her abilities to manage BogLand.

Sometimes, she still just wanted to be a simple ol'

country girl again, and spend her days growing a garden and cooking from scratch. Establishing BogLand had intervened for a decade, but now, in spite of their advancing age, they both wanted a couple of children. Sally felt her abdomen and, oblivious to her own choice of words, wondered which gender this tadpole would be. She planned to taper off her engagement with BogLand as they grew and gradually return to comforting homestead activities and teaching the kids how to be self-sufficient.

Grace whispered in Johnny's ear. "It's still hard for me to come here."

"I know, me too," and held her closer.

Love Wanders did not remember much about the long eons of entrapment in the grove. Except for his dull aching longing for Waits, the passage of time mostly seemed like an interminable stupor. What he did recall consisted of vague impressions: darkness, dampness, profound silence, fecundity, and the slow growth of roots and ground-flesh filaments. Once a year, during the autumnal rains, he could experience the aboveground world of light and rain through the ground-fleshes that emerged. Those few days each year flashed by as the mushrooms engaged in frenzied sex before decomposing back into the ground. It was during these annual interludes that he could most keenly sense the nearby trapped and agonized spirit of Waits for Love. They yearned hopelessly for each other across the unyielding gulf of the shaman's curse. When Love's awareness melted back into the soil each winter, he inevitably felt guilty that he welcomed the renewed stupor while Waits continued to suffer almost daily.

It's like eating some mushroom that makes you ill to

your stomach, Waits for Grace thought to herself. If you don't force yourself to try mushrooms again, your aversion will become ingrained and you will never again be able to savor them. OK, well, that might be stretching the analogy a little, but Love and I met here, on this very spot, millennia ago! We sealed our tryst here, and now Ole, Sally, and Johnny all love to come here for the anniversary celebrations of our dual weddings. Love knows how this place still haunts my dreams. He understands how I suffered almost continuous misery and loneliness because I could partially materialize in the morning and evening fog or mist to sense my surroundings. He comprehends how I still feel the greater guilt for convincing him to eat the shaman's jumping ground-fleshes with me. Love is so kind and patient now. He does not force me to come here, but he is right that I need to supplant the negative memories with a long string of new positive ones. So, how about another good one, she decided.

"It's getting dark," Grace broke their silent contemplation with a soft, but eager voice, "how about the toast!"

"You betcha," Ole agreed. "Sally, would you hand me the picnic basket please?"

Meanwhile Johnny had fetched the traditional basket Mary had woven for them as an appropriate container for her secret wedding gift. While Ole retrieved a rare bottle of Bert's Stankovich '44, Grace nimbly lifted out the two doeskin-wrapped items and gave one to Sally. The women carefully unwrapped the precious whale-skull bone chalices that were already acquiring a lovely light rose hue from cranberry wine stains of the previous nine shared anniversaries.

"Has Mary confided in you the tale of these marvelous treasures yet?" Sally inquired.

"Not yet," Grace said, "but I suspect she will one day soon, when the time is right. Meanwhile, she just drops hints like 'whales need thick skulls to hold their immense intelligence and long memories,' or 'whales know the dark depths but also enjoy living now under the bright blue sky,' or other such cryptic comments about vessels for sentience or unfathomable experiences. The one thing she does repeat is her admonition to 'honor them, as well as ourselves, with our rituals.' I know we all concur on that one." They did.

Ole filled the two chalices. Sally hoisted hers and, without knowing the full import of her chosen words, said, "To love that lingers forever!"

Love Wanders had his arm around his mate's shoulder and he felt her wince slightly. Grace showed no other sign of her reaction and paused for only a moment.

After they all had sipped the first toast, she lifted her chalice and proposed: "To never waiting again!" They all could, and did, drink to that!

Love and Waits were never reluctant to leave the bog. The anniversary celebrations were starting to become a treasured tradition, but each time they left, they felt like it was definitely time to go. The growing darkness had little to do with their impatience. It seemed more as if awakened tendrils had started reaching for them again, searching for a connection from long habit.

The engendered bog/grove/fungus/spirit entity that imbued this insular bulb of reality with awareness could not be said to have emotions. Put into human terms, one might say it perceived a void or incompleteness where the departing guest spirits had long dwelled. No matter. The synthiant now remained assured of its continued existence.

Inadvertently lingering, Grace brought up the rear as they left sight of the bog in the descending darkness. She nervously glanced back one more time at the fog condensing just above the surface of the bog. Yes! He was still there! She shivered violently, turned quickly, and dashed after the others.

Bats began weaving a crisscross pattern of looping flights above the bog. The current resident owl hooted. The bog fog thickened in the dusk.

Hardly visible, barely more than an illusion, there floated the pale stooped-over figure of a very, very, very, old man drifting soundlessly, aimlessly. His wraithlike form smoldered faintly with the pallid shimmering tints of an icy northern night sky.

Longevity might not mean immortality, but long ages have yet to pass before the last bitter bog spirit fades away.

###

David Pilz and George McAdams

Notes

Regarding this book

This novel is fictional and was written for enjoyment. The core ideas, key characters and basic plot were devised in the minds of us two white guys during an evening of brainstorming with a bottle of good wine around a campfire while exploring the southern Oregon coast in May of 2001. The context and general elements of the tale are derived from real settings we encountered or research we subsequently conducted, but specific material was invented to flesh out the story. The first author is soley responsible for any errors.

Regarding the Native American Indian tribes in this book:

When and how peoples from northeast Asia migrated into North America is still debated. Likely there were multiple migrations by various routes. Coastal migration routes were used even at the height of the ice ages, but evidence of this migration, or of settlements en route are now mostly under seas that rose when the Pleistocene glaciers melted. In any case, the continent's first immigrants were likely living on what is now the Oregon coast by 15,000 or more years ago.

According to William C. Sturtevant [1990. Handbook of North American Indians. Volume 7: Northwest Coast. Washington, D.C.: Smithsonian Institution] when Europeans showed up, the inhabitants of the area where this novel takes place were recorded by early chroniclers to be the Kwatami band (also spelled Quatomah, meaning "people of the inside water"). They were a band of the Tututni Group of the Athapaskan tribes of southwestern Oregon. Members of the nearby Upper Coquille Tribe called themselves the Mishikhwutmetunne, meaning "people dwelling on the river Mishi" (the Coquille River).

The U.S. Government eventually restored the Coquille Tribe to officially recognized status in 1989.

The Coquille Tribe used to advertise production of organic, hand picked cranberries, under the business name, "Coquille Cranberries." However, as of April 20, 2010, this name was listed as "not renewed" on the Oregon Secretary of State Corporation Division website. References to the business also have been removed from the Tribe's business web site: http://www.cedco.net. That said, I was able to buy some Coquille Tribe dried cranberries at my local food cooperative in 2013. They were delicious.

Coquille tribal headquarters are located in North Bend, OR. http://www.coquilletribe.org

The Tribal Library has numerous resources for individuals interested in further pursuing their actual history and culture. http://www.coquilletribe.org/citlibrary.htm

The tribe also operates The Mill Casino and Hotel in Coos Bay, OR. http://www.themillcasino.com

Regarding the fungi in this book:

Two fungi have been revered in Eurasian history as "mushrooms of immortality" and both types are included in our storyline.

In Asia, this term has been applied to the medicinal conk (*Ganoderma lucidum*) called "Reishi" in Japan or "Ling Chi" in China. It is prized for its invigorating and life-extending properties. Paul Stamets provides a succinct review of this fungus in his treatise, "MycoMedicinals." It doesn't really induce extreme longevity, so we shifted the fanciful identity of our conk to a very rare fungus genus that colonizes ancient *Chamaecyparis* trees in the eastern United States. No species of this genus are known to grow on western U.S. *Chamaecyparis* species (for instance, coastal Oregon Port-Orford cedars), but after all, this is fiction. The fungal genus in question is *Echinodontium*. For more information see the Shernoff 2007 article listed below.

In India and Russia, *Amanita muscaria*, the fly agaric was termed the "mushroom of immortality" for its psychoactive properties by R. Gordon Wasson in his book entitled Soma: Divine Mushroom of Immortality where he postulated it was the divine "soma" of the ancient Vedic text, the Rig Veda.

Although recent genetic analyses suggest that most North American fungi are distinct from similar species on other continents, we hint at the assumption that the shaman recognized unique, extremely potent strains of both of these "mushrooms of immortality" that grew on the Pacific shores of both eastern Asian and western North American coasts. That unique strains of such fungi exist is not an unreasonable assumption. See collection # FB-30986 (CBM) of a unique *Amanita muscaria* specimen sampled in Japan as cited in the Oda et. al. 2004 journal article listed below.

Paul Stamets first explicitly postulated the concept that fungal mycelial networks could embody a form of intelligence or sentience in his book, Mycelium Running. We allude to this notion, especially toward the end.

References

Millman L. (2013). In Search of an Extinct Polypore. In: Giant Polypores & Stoned Reindeer. Cambridge, MA: Komatik Press. pp. 70-76.

Oda, Takashi; Tanaka, Chihiro; Tsuda, Mitsuya. 2004. Molecular phylogeny and biogeography of the widely distributed Amanita species, *A. muscaria* and *A. pantherina.* Molecular Research. 108(8): 885-896.

Shernoff, Leon. Fall 2007. A real American ivory-billed woodpecker: *Echinodontium ballouii* rediscovered. Mushroom, The Journal of Wild Mushrooming. Issue 97, Vol. 25, Number 4, pp. 13-15, 19-25.

Stamets, P.; Yao, C.D.W. 2002. MycoMedicinals: an informational treatise on mushrooms. Olympia, WA: MycoMedia Productions. 96 p.

Stamets, P. 2005. Mycelium Running: How Mushrooms Can Help Save The World. Berkeley: Ten Speed Press. 340 p.

Wasson, R. Gordon. 1968. Soma: Divine Mushroom of Immortality. Ethno-Mycological Studies 1. New York: Harcourt Brace Jovanovich, Inc. 380 p.

Regarding the geology and vegetation of natural bogs in the area:

Our character, Twarn, in the book describes much regarding the vegetation, geology and etiology of coastal dunes and bogs of the area of the southern Oregon Coast where the story is set.

While camping in the area, the authors explored small ponds edged with the insectivorous "pitcher" plant *Darlingtonia californica* and lined with Port Orford cedars (*Chamaecyparis lawsoniana*) trees. In the course of our explorations, we also discovered a highly unusual cluster of small oaks (about 20+ clustered stems, 10 feet high, and with a rounded canopy) on the edge of one of these ponds. I tentatively identified these oaks as a disjunct population of the *Quercus garryana* (Oregon white oak) variety *breweri*, but the online Flora of North America suggests that coastal populations of such oaks are likely stunted forms of the Oregon White oak or hybrids with the leather oak (*Quercus durata*), a species that grows in nutrient poor soils such as bogs. In this novel, we postulate that the unusual coastal dune-bog oaks are hybrids with the deer oak (*Quercus sadleriana*) that grows in the nearby Siskiyou Mountains, because unlike any other West Coast oak, the closest living relative of the deer oak is Asian. This fits well with the hypothetical mycorrhizal association that the oaks in our grove have with an unusual strain of *Amanita muscaria* also found in Asia.

References

Atwater, Brian F.; Satoko, Musumi-Rokkaku; Kenji,

Satake; Yoshinobu, Tsuji; Kazue, Ueda; Yamaguchi, David K. 2005. The Orphan Tsunami of 1700: Japanese Clues to a Parent Earthquake in North America. Seattle: University of Washington Press. 133 pages.

Christy, John A. 1979. Report on a preliminary survey of Sphagnum-containing wetlands of the Oregon Coast. Salem, OR: Natural Area Preserves Advisory Committee report to the Oregon State Land Board, Division of State Lands.

Flora of North America Editorial Committee, eds. 1993+. Flora of North America North of Mexico. 19+ vols. New York and Oxford. http://floranorthamerica.org

Hansen, Henry P. 1943. Paleoecology of two sand dune bogs on the southern Oregon Coast. American Journal of Botany. 30(5): 335-340

Pavlik, Bruce M.; Muick, Pamela C.; Johnson, Sharon, Popper, Marjorie. 1991. Oaks of California. Los Olivos, CA: Cachuma Press, Inc. 184 pages.

Riggs, George B. 1925. Some Sphagnum bogs of the North Pacific Coast of America. Ecology. 6(3): 260-279.

U.S. Department of the Interior, Bureau of Land Management. Updated May 2004. New River Area of Critical Environmental Concern (ACEC) Management Plan. Myrtlewood Field Office, Coos Bay District. Document: BLM/OR/WA/PL-04/032-1792 available from Coos Bay District Office, 1300 Airport Lane, North Bend, OR 97459.

Regarding the cranberry industry of the southern Oregon coast:

Cranberries are an important agricultural crop on the southern Oregon coast, especially in the low-lying flatlands that are interior from coastal dunes between Coos Bay and Cape Blanco (just north of Port Orford).

The centrally located city in this area, Bandon, really does have an annual Cranberry festival. They celebrate their 70th anniversary of the festival September 9, 10, & 11, 2016. It includes a Food Fair, live music and a Cranberry Court coronation, among other activities. See the events calendar at http://www.bandon.com

The equivalent of our book's Cranberry Farmer's Association is the real-life Oregon Cranberry Growers Association: http://www.oregoncranberrygrowers.com.

Actually, before we knew they existed, we conceived of the association, the festival and the queen while originally brainstorming the story around the campfire. The names have been changed in our book to protect our innocence.

References

Eck, Paul. 2005. The American Cranberry. New Brunswick: Rutgers University Press. 420 p.

Regarding the "Got Mold?" business name.

We noticed a sign with this business name while driving through one of the towns on the southern Oregon coast. It is listed on the website of the Oregon Secretary of State

Corporation Division. The business name was not renewed as of July 17, 2006.

Regarding the section-separating glyph

The character used to divide sections within a chapter is a runic character derived from the Proto-Norse alphabet called Elder Futhark dating to the 2nd to 8th centuries. The character (reconstructed as "eihwaz") is the Proto-Germanic word for "yew." The character was copied from the Wikimedia Commons at: https://commons.wikimedia.org/w/index.php?curid=7252 81